I've Found Her

Joy Mullett

To my friends and family who have always believed me.
To you, the reader, thank you for giving my work a chance.
To the universe, for making my dreams come true.

Authors Note

Please be aware this book contains sexual content and graphic language, it is intended for mature audiences ages 18 and over.

The story includes some darker themes, including kidnapping, domestic violence and murder.

However, the real focus is on romance and a hero alpha male.

If you are ok with this, please continue and enjoy!

Prologue

Damien

Have you ever had the feeling you have forgotten something? Or you are looking for something, but cannot for the life of you remember what it is? It's as if something is missing, and there is an empty void that needs to be filled. Do you ever get a wave of homesickness when you are in the very place you call home?

I do, and it infuriates me.

I am constantly searching for this missing piece of my puzzle. Sometimes I'm between consciousness and sleep when I see what it is I am looking for, and for a split second, I feel an overwhelming relief and a sense of being home and fulfilled. But, as quickly as the second arrives, it disappears and so does the memory of what I had seen. I then quickly become fully conscious and have absolutely no recollection of what I just saw. I remember that I saw it, and I remember how I felt, but it's gone.

I don't remember when or why this feeling started, but I know when it ends.

It ends when **I've Found Her.**

Chapter 1

Bella

Staring out of the train window, I'm mesmerised by the trees and buildings that whizz past so fast, creating colourful stripes and patterns. I try to focus on the beauty it makes rather than my increased heart rate, sweaty palms, and the bile that threatens to escape my stomach.

My phone alerts me to a WhatsApp message.

John: YOU'RE MAKING A MISTAKE BELLA. COME HOME!!

My homesickness begins to subside at the reminder of why I am relocating and pushing myself to follow my dream. After deleting the message, I go on to my emails and reread the job offer I received, for about the hundredth time:

From: Rebecca@foster&thomas.co.uk

Dear Bella White,

I am pleased to offer you the position of senior stylist at the Foster & Thomas salon at Trinity King.

We were very impressed with you on your trial day, you fit in with the team well, and we believe your skills will be an asset to the Foster & Thomas family.

I hope that you accept the offer. I understand that it will mean relocating for yourself, but I am sure I do not need to explain what an incredible opportunity this is.

As we spoke about in your interview, the position comes with many benefits, one of which is accommodation. You will find all the benefits and details of your position in the attached document.

I look forward to hearing from you.

Kind regards,

Rebecca Thomas.

The email gives me the boost that I need, and I relax a little, feeling excited about my new start.

The senior stylist position I have accepted is in one of London's top hair salons. Foster & Thomas is situated in one of London's finest hotels, Trinity by King. The hotel is on Trinity Square and is one of many of the five-star King hotels. The chain has hotels all over the world. I hadn't been inside one until the day I went for my job trial. It was breathtaking. The way it smelt stays in my memory the most. As soon as I entered those revolving doors, my senses were hit with the sweetest, freshest fragrance I had ever come across. Apparently, it's the King hotel's signature scent for all their hotels. No wonder the chain is so popular. Foster & Thomas is any stylist's dream employer. How I, Bella White, from a small town in the middle of nowhere, have managed to land a job there is little short of a miracle. But I believe in miracles, in dreams and fairy tales, and this miracle arose at the perfect time.

Thinking back, I've lived a very normal, sheltered life up to now. I grew up in a lovely little village where everyone knew everyone. I had the perfect childhood. I was raised in a loving family and lived in a modest home with my mother and father, where I wanted for nothing. I went to the local schools and always had lots of friends. When I left school, I wanted to be a hairdresser. My parents encouraged me to follow my heart and would have stuck by me whatever I had chosen. I worked at 'Joyce's', my local salon, from the time I was fourteen. I started as the Saturday girl and worked my way up to being a senior stylist. I loved it. I worked so hard getting all the qualifications I could and attending course after course in the latest techniques. Unfortunately, I didn't get to use these techniques very often. The only time I did was when I convinced one of my friends to be my guinea pig. It was a typical shampoo-and-set type of salon, nothing very exciting. I've always wanted to do so much more.

Recently I attended a colour training course in London. One of the girls on the course said she worked at Foster & Thomas and that she was emigrating a month later. I googled the salon on my train ride home. The job opening was advertised on their website, and for some reason, I filled out the application form.

I received the job offer email from Rebecca one week ago. Now I am on the 7:00 a.m. train to Euston, London. I have my suitcase, my handbag, and an extremely sick feeling in the pit of my stomach. The past week has felt like a blur. I've been so busy sorting everything out, I haven't had a chance to stop and think. Am I doing the right thing? I'll soon find out, and if it doesn't work out, I can *"get straight back on that train and come home,"* in the words of my father. This is just what I need, a fresh start on my own.

When the train arrives at Euston, my anxiety kicks in with full force. I now must get on the tube. London is so busy. I've never seen so many people in one place. Everyone is rushing around, talking on phones. If you stop moving, you are sure to get knocked over. I take a deep breath and exit the train.

Following the signs in the station, I make my way to the underground. It isn't my first time in London, but I don't think I'll ever get used to it. It is so different to home. I quickly text my parents and my best friend Chloe to let them know I've arrived at Euston and that I am about to get the tube. I check the map and find the line to take me to Tower Hill. The tube station is only a short walk from the hotel, a "stone's throw," as Rebecca said (she obviously hasn't seen me try and throw a ball). I stand, checking and double-checking the line to make sure I have the right one. Once I'm sure, I stand and wait on the platform. It quickly fills up with people pushing and shoving to be closest to the yellow line. The first time I came to London and used the tube, I was so overwhelmed. I was frozen to the platform. I watched four trains go past before I built up the courage and pushed my way on.

I stand tall, ready for the rush as the train pulls up. Holding my case with as much confidence as I can muster, I jump on. Unfortunately, I always worry about things, but I try not to let it stop me doing want I want. Pretty much holding my breath the entire journey, I count the stations until my stop.

When I'm finally outside the tube station, breathing in the cool, fresh air, I'm proud of myself for getting here. I check my phone maps, taking a moment to get my bearings and allow my breathing and heart rate to steady. Once I'm certain of the direction I need to go, I set off walking through the busy streets of London. While I walk, I ring my mum. I'm so happy to hear her voice, even though I saw her waving me off at the station only a few hours ago.

"Hello, sweetheart. Have you arrived safely?" she asks.

"Yes, I'm here, safe and sound." I reply, relieved the journey is over.

"I am so glad. We are so proud of you sweetie. Now you go and show them how wonderful you are. Call us later when you have settled in. We love you, Bella," Mum and Dad say in unison. They always have their phone on loudspeaker so they can both hear me.

"Love you too—speak later," I say, then hang up.

As I walk, I take in the city around me. The buildings are big and striking, and the roads are full of bright-red double-decker buses and taxis beeping their horns. I've never felt so far away from home, but I'm also so exhilarated. I smile to myself, excited to see what awaits me in my new chapter. My phone pings, alerting me that I've arrived at my destination.

Taking a deep breath, I look up at the impressive building that I will now call home. With my head held high and butterflies in my stomach, I walk into the King Hotel.

Chapter 2

Damien

"Mr. King, my deepest condolences. Your father was a great man. I am honoured I could call him a friend as well as client. Today is not the time, but we do need to arrange a meeting to get your father's affairs in order. As you are now the owner of the King enterprise, you need to decide whether you will be taking over as CEO or if you will be appointing someone to take on that role. Either way, the position needs to be filled momentarily. I'll be in touch."

"I'm sure you will, Mr. Davis."

We shake hands, and I turn to get into my waiting car. George, my driver, gives me a gentle nod through his rear-view mirror and sets off, leaving me to gather my thoughts.

It has been a long-ass day. A long couple of weeks, actually. I am mentally and physically drained. All I can think about is getting home and having a scotch. My father's passing came as a shock, especially so soon after my mother. But even the best doctor's money can buy can't mend a broken heart. He will be happy he is back with my mother now. And at least I got to have him live here with me in New York for his final days.

My car pulls into the basement parking of my apartment building. George opens my door, and I step out.

"Thank you, George. You may retire for the evening now," I say.

"Thank you, sir. I shall see you in the morning."

I step into my private lift and make my way up to the penthouse where I have lived for the past ten years. I'm used to the city life now, but it's a lot different from my hometown in England.

Standing in my kitchen, I pour myself a drink and look out over central park at the New York skyline. It is getting dark, and the view is spectacular. While sipping my scotch and watching the evening light show of the city, my mind wanders to my parents and their love and devotion to each other. Family was everything to them—that and the King enterprise, which came a close second, much to my mum's annoyance. But everything my Dad did was for me and my mum. It was a very rare love they shared. I don't think I have ever seen it in anyone else. They always said they were soulmates, if that's even a thing. My parents always believed there is one special person for everyone. I, however, do not have this belief. I'm perfectly happy on my own, having no one to please but myself. Past relationships have been complicated, and well, let's just say I will not be entering in any form of a relationship anytime soon.

After a few more drinks, my head starts to clear, and I know what I need to do. I pick up my phone and call my best friend and business partner, Josh.

Josh answers on the first ring. "Damien, how are you? Sorry I couldn't be there today. How did it go?"

"As well as can be expected. Dad's ashes will be ready for me to collect tomorrow in time for me to take them to England. And no apologies necessary. I appreciate all you have been doing with the business, taking on my role as well as yours."

"Don't mention it. Anything I can do to help."

"Well, that's why I called. I know I said I would only be in England for a few days, but I've decided to step into my father's shoes, only for a while. The King hotel chain wasn't just his business, it was also his family, and I want to make sure it's taken care of properly," I explain.

"Whatever you need to do," he assures me. "I have everything covered. We are taking on new staff, we have new offices, and business is booming. You haven't had any time off since we set up King Security all those years ago. You take all the time you need. Plus, it's not like you do much anyway." Josh laughs.

After catching up with Josh, I email Mr.

Davies, my dad's and now my solicitor, to inform him of what I have decided. He immediately replies and sends me over the paperwork I have requested.

I finish my drink and head to bed.

The next morning, I collect my dad's ashes and board my private jet to England to lay my dad to rest next to my mum.

During the flight, I go through some of the paperwork Mr. Davies sent me. I'm overwhelmed with emotion as I read what my father has achieved in his lifetime. Forty years ago, he opened his first King Hotel. Since then, he's turned the King name into a chain of 600 hotels across six continents. My dad thought of all his staff as family. He would treat the cleaner with the same respect as the manager and paid them all well. I'm overcome with pride as I read about his accomplishments.

I find my father's last to-do list and decide this would be a good place to start. It seems there have been some issues at the Trinity Hotel in London. It has a significantly high workforce turnover, and my father wanted to find out why. Luckily England is where I am currently heading, so I decided to stay there for my time in London rather than in my family home. I haven't had much to do with the hotels previously, but my dad always made sure he knew what was going on and made his presence felt in them as often as he could.

I want to continue this as much as my schedule will allow.

"Mr. King, we shall be landing in an hour. George will have the car ready to take you to Kingston Manor as soon as we arrive. Is there anywhere you would like to go on the way?" asks my assistant Penny.

"Actually, I have decided to stay at the Trinity. There are a few things I would like to get to the bottom of. Please make a reservation, but not in my name. I want to observe the operation's performance without getting any special treatment," I respond.

"Good idea, sir. I shall let George know, and I will arrange the reservation. Will Damien 'Smith' suffice?" she replies.

"Yes, that will be fine. Thank you, Penny."

Penny is more than just my personal assistant. She is also George's wife. Penny and George have worked for my family since I was a boy. They both moved over to New York with me and are more like family to me than employees.

A couple of hours later, I walk through the revolving doors of Trinity by King. I smile to myself as its signature smell brings back fond memories of my mother. It smells just like her —the sweetness of strawberries and freshness of apple. It was her idea to have all the hotels smelling the same; my father just let her run with it. He'd do anything to make her happy. It was, in fact, a very good idea. The King scent is now a brand of its own.

"Good evening, Mr. Smith. Welcome to Trinity by King. Your driver let me know you were arriving. One of the bell boys is with him now and will ensure your luggage gets to your room. My name is Tiffany, and I'll be here until 8:00 tonight. If there is anything I can do for you, Mr. Smith, please let me know," she says, fluttering her eye lashes and leaning closer towards me. "Will you be staying with us alone, or will someone be joining you?" She runs her fingers through her hair while pushing her chest together with her arms.

"I will be staying alone. Therefore, I will only need the one room key. I am sure the key allocation was the reason you were asking?" My reply is stern and dismissive.

Tiffany has dark hair, brown eyes, olive skin, and a pretty smile. I know that if I want, I can have her in my bed just after eight. I'm no stranger to having women throw themselves at me. Sometimes I do take them up on their offer. A man has needs after all, but today I'm in no frame of mind to entertain anyone. Especially not playful and flirtatious Tiffany.

As Tiffany continues her laughable seduction, my attention is caught by a beautiful young woman. She has a presence about her that makes her impossible to ignore.

Standing at about five foot five and wearing jeans that hug her curves perfectly with a top that hangs loosely off her shoulders, she is slim but curvy in all the right places. She catches my full attention. I'm drawn to her exposed sun-kissed skin. I imagine what it would be like to kiss that flawless skin of hers. Suddenly, she turns quickly, as if her skin can feel my eyes upon it. Looking directly at me, her bright blue eyes look straight into mine as if seeing into my soul. The encounter sends ripples of warmth down my body. Ripples which make my cock stir. What is it about her? After seconds of eye contact, she shivers, then turns, swishing her long golden hair as she goes. She disappears into the staff quarters entrance, pulling a bright yellow case behind her, leaving me with a strange emptiness.

Chapter 3

Bella

I make my way through the foyer. My instructions are to go to the staff quarters entrance situated to the right of the lobby. I'm to take the lift to housekeeping on the fifth floor and ask for Katie, who is also a stylist at Foster & Thomas. As I walk through the beautiful reception area, I am overcome with the strangest feeling that I am being watched. When I turn to investigate, my eyes are instantly met with the most attractive man I have ever seen. He's tall—he must be over six feet. An expensive-looking tracksuit clings to every curve of his large muscular frame. His hair is dark, almost black, and short on the sides but long enough on the top to be swept back. A light stubble perfectly frames his strong jaw line. His dark brown eyes widen as I look into them, and their warmth sends tingles through my skin. I shiver in response. Shocked by the way my body responds to this man, I quickly continue to where I am supposed to be.

Stepping out of the lift, I am greeted by a girl about my age with bright pink hair and perfectly done makeup. She gives me the biggest welcoming smile.

"Hi! You must be Bella. I'm Katie. I am so happy to meet you!" She envelops me in a big hug, which immediately puts me at ease. "Come on—let me give you a tour."

Katie shows me around housekeeping. We pick up some towels and bedding for my room, and she explains where I can do my laundry. We meet a few people on our way, and Katie introduces me to them. Everyone seems very friendly. My room is on the next floor up. Katie's is just next door, which I'm really pleased about. Together we make my bed, and then Katie helps me unpack my things. I haven't brought much; at home, I pretty much lived in jeans, jumpers, and trainers. My uniform at work was a black tunic and trousers—nothing like what hair stylists wear in London. Everyone here dresses to the current trends. My plan is to see what everyone else is wearing and go shopping for a new wardrobe as soon as possible.

My room is great. On one side, it has a double bed with bedside tables and a large wardrobe with drawers inside. Next to that is a huge window with a beautiful view of Trinity Square Gardens. On the other side of the room is a modern but compact kitchen, a two-seater sofa in the corner, and a television on the wall. In the centre of the room is a door leading to the shared bathroom. Thankfully the room that adjoins it is Katie's, but sharing with someone I have only just met still makes me anxious.

"I'll leave you settle in, Bella. Me and the rest of the team are going out for drinks tonight. You should come along. It will be a great opportunity for you to meet everyone before you start work. You'll come, won't you?" Katies asks persuasively.

"Oh, I'm not sure. I'm really tired after my journey, and I need to call my family and let them know I've arrived here safely."

"That's okay. We aren't meeting until 7:00, so you can have a rest and make your phone calls first. I'll knock for you at about five to, okay?"

Without giving me a chance to protest, Katie leaves, closing the door behind her.

Flopping down on my bed in exhaustion, I feel a little homesick. Thankfully before my thoughts turn negative, my phone rings. Its Chloe.

"Bella! How are you? How's your room? Are you okay? Is everyone being nice to you?" Chloe says, making me laugh—she always looks out for me. It is really strange being so far away from each other.

"I'm good! Katie, one of the other stylists met me and showed me around a bit. Then she helped me unpack and sort out my room. She's invited me out tonight with a few of the other guys from the salon. We are meeting in about an hour. I'm not sure where we are going. It will be nice to get to know everyone, I hope they like me."

"That's great. I'm glad you're settling in. Of course they will like you—don't be daft! A night out sounds like just what you need. What are you going to wear?" she asks. I hadn't really given that much thought. I didn't have much to choose from really. I'd brought my best black jeans and a couple of lace tops; that would have to do.

Chatting to Chloe for a while makes me feel better. I promise to call her tomorrow with the night's gossip. After freshening up, I put a few more curls in my hair and apply some natural makeup. I'm ready in my jeans and top when Katie knocks on the door. She looks stunning. Her pink hair is long and thick with extensions, and her makeup is much heavier than mine. She looks gorgeous. Katie's short, sparkly navy dress and barely-there stilettos make me feel very underdressed.

"Would you like to borrow something of mine, Bella? We are about the same size, and I have a few dresses that will suit you perfectly."

Before I can answer, Katie ushers me into her room, where she rummages through her wardrobe, holding out various dresses and putting them up against me. We settle on a black one-shoulder dress. It is a little shorter than I'd usually wear, but I must admit, it makes me look good. Katie also gives me a similar pair of shoes to the ones she is wearing.

A little while later, we walk into the bar, and I instantly know which group we are meeting. They give off this fabulous aura. I feel a flutter of excitement; tonight is going to be a good night.

The group is so friendly and welcoming. My concerns that they may not like me are soon forgotten. I can be shy at first, which some people mistake for ignorance. Worrying too much about what people think of me has me reluctant to talk. But I need not have been worried—they all have me relaxed from the start. Each of my new work colleagues introduces themselves. There's Nick the hair extensions specialist and his partner Joe, Sarah the receptionist, and James the colour expert. They're all immaculate—hair, makeup, clothes—each one with their own unique style. I am in awe of them all. We're all chatting and laughing when we are suddenly interrupted.

"Hello, guys! Fancy seeing you here. I hope you're not making too much noise and making the guests feel uncomfortable?!" a gravelly voice interjects.

The group all pull faces and roll their eyes at one another. Nick then turns with a false smile to face the man who has just approached us.

"Graham, how lovely to see you," he says in a sarcastic way.

"It's Mr. Graham to you, Nick," says the man who looks like he works at the hotel. Then the man catches sight of me, and he comes over to stand right beside me.

"Well, hello there. I haven't met you before—what is your name?"

Katie instinctively grabs my arm and pulls me towards her.

"She's with us, and we were just leaving, weren't we guys?" she responds protectively, picking up her bag and pulling me towards the door.

The group quickly follows, and we leave before I can say anything. I have to practically run to keep up with them, and these shoes definitely aren't made for running in! We exit the hotel and enter a nearby Wetherspoons just a few doors down.

"So, who was that, Katie? I get the impression you don't like him?" I ask.

"Don't like him, ha, that's the understatement of the century! He's the biggest slimeball you will ever meet. So many girls have left because of him. I don't fully know what happened to them, but I can guess. I'm not talking just a couple either. I'm talking tens of girls just in the past two years I've worked here." She shudders visibly, clearly feeling repulsed.

"Why doesn't someone report him? Surely that's a sackable offence, not to mention illegal." I exclaim.

"Some of the girls have tried, but unfortunately, he is the manager of Trinity by King. So, his word is stronger than theirs. Just stay away from him, Bella. If he says or does anything that makes you uncomfortable, tell me straight away, promise?" she instructs.

"Yes, I will," I reply obediently. Katie reminds me so much of Chloe. Always having my back.

The drinks have been flowing for a few hours. We've worked our way through the cocktail list, and I am having so much fun. I have not stopped laughing. The guys decide it's time for dancing. We leave Wetherspoons and head to a bar that is apparently *The* place to dance. We settle at a table near the dance floor and order a round of drinks.

I excuse myself and make my way to the toilet. All these cocktails have gone straight through me as well as to my head. I'm feeling a little tipsy, but I'm still in control. Once I'm all freshened up, I leave the toilets. I'm on my way back to our table when I feel a sweaty hand grab my shoulder. I turn to see the owner of the sticky body, and my heart sinks. Mr. Graham. I scan the area around me to see if I can see anyone I know. Unfortunately, I'm out of sight from our table. I'm in a quiet, dark area of the bar. Only people coming to use the toilets would see me.

"Hello, beautiful—I'm glad I've caught you. I want to introduce myself. My name is Mr. Graham, and I am the manager of Trinity. So I am, so to speak, your boss," the smarmy man says, far closer to my face than I'd like. I can smell the alcohol and garlic on his breath.

I hold in a gag. "Yes, I know who you are. It's nice to meet you, but I really need to get back to my friends." Moving away from him doesn't work. He catches my arm and holds tight.

"Not so fast, young lady. I'm not finished

with you yet. You need to remember who I am. I can make your time working for us as enjoyable or as painful as I wish."

I feel sick as he comes closer to me and continues, "I have a fully stocked minibar in my penthouse apartment. It has a fabulous view of the city," he whispers while stroking my arm. "I am sure that dress of yours would look wonderful on my bedroom floor." Graham laughs at his own joke, moving his body uncomfortably closer to mine.

I try and move further into the bar where someone might see us. But he manoeuvres me against the wall. I mentally beg someone to come to the toilet and intervene. But nobody does. It's the same old story, and I know fighting it will only make it worse.

"Please, Mr. Graham. My friends will be wondering where I am. How about tomorrow—we could get drinks?"

A frown crosses his brow, and for a moment, I think he might let me go.

"Why put off till tomorrow what we can do today. You're coming with me." Mr. Graham puts his arm around my shoulders and forcibly directs me towards the exit.

"No! I am not going with you." My feet press into the floor, and my body stiffens in protest against moving. The anger in his face has me tensed and ready for a beating. But it doesn't come.

Out of nowhere, a pair of big strong hands grab Mr. Graham's arms and throw him to the floor at force.

"The lady said NO!" bellows a deep voice.

Standing in disbelief, I watch as Graham struggles to get back on to his feet. The tall, dark, muscular hero picks him up by his shirt and escorts him to the nearest security guard. My hero then returns and asks me how I am. That is when I realise that it is the guy I saw in the lobby when I arrived at the hotel earlier today. My body reacts the same way it did then. Tingles and warm pulses spread all over my skin.

"Thank you" is all I can bring myself to say.

He looks at me with a dark, heated desire. His gaze runs down my body and back up to my eyes.

"Did he hurt you?" he demands.

"Not really—just scared me a bit, that's all," I reply.

He relaxes a little. "I'm Damien, and your name is?"

"Bella."

"It is a pleasure to make your acquaintance, Bella."

The way Damien says my name makes me warm inside. He speaks very well with a London English accent. His voice is deep and rough. His eyes are dark and alluring. I could get lost in them. He smells fresh and manly. But most surprisingly, I feel comfortable and safe near him. His hand rests on my shoulder. I shiver at his touch. Damien quickly removes it, obviously thinking he has overstepped.

"It's fine. I'm just a little anxious after what happened," I lie. I allow my eyes to linger on his lips, imagining what they would feel like on mine.

A small smile begins to spread across them as if he knows what I am thinking.

"Can I escort you to your boyfriend? Your friend? Who are you with tonight?" Damien asks as he scans the bar.

"I don't have a boyfriend, and my friends are just over there. I'm sure I will be fine now. Thank you so much for your help with everything, but I really must be getting back to them. They will be wondering where I am. It was lovely to meet you, Damien, and thanks again," I say, then turn in the direction of our table.

"As you wish, Miss White, and the pleasure was all mine," he replies.

As I go to walk away, I realise I didn't give Damien my last name. I turn back to ask him how he knew, but he has disappeared. I go back to the table and sit down next to Katie, I fill her in on the excitement I had on my way back from the toilet.

"I am never letting you out of my sight again!" she exclaims.

On Sunday morning, I wake up with a fuzzy head. Having had such a good night, I don't regret how I feel. We laughed and danced the whole night. The group welcomed me warmly, and I already feel like one of the team.

I then think about my encounter with Damien, and it still baffles me how he knew my surname. I replay him effortlessly getting Graham away from me, remembering the way he looked at me and how he made me feel. I have never felt like that around a man before. During all the years I'd been with John—even in the beginning before things went bad—not once had he sent tingles down my body by just looking at me.

Speak of the devil—my phone pings with a message:

John: BELLA I AM SORRY RING ME PLEASE.

John messages me every day. Sometimes his messages are apologetic, and sometimes they are angry. Sometimes I reply, and sometimes I don't. Hopefully now that I have moved away, he will leave me alone. I'm in two minds on whether to block his number again. London is a bit far for him to just turn up. Then again, I wouldn't put it past him.

Bella: Thank you for your apology, John. I am sorry you are hurting, but you need to move on. I am starting a new life in London. It is the best thing for both of us. I really care about you, John, and I hope that we can be friends.

John: FRIENDS?! You are going to be my wife! You have proved your point. Now come home!

I decide not to reply again. John is obviously still very hurt, and I don't want him to get more upset. I just hope that in time, he will accept that I've left him and move on.

I spend all morning in bed. I ring Chloe and tell her all about my night. Chloe advises me to stay clear of all men at the minute. She's right; I came here to concentrate on my career, not to fall into the arms of another man. Damien's arms. His big, toned arms that could pick me up and... *Bella, stop!* I really need to get my mind in check, what is going on with me?

I spend the afternoon getting to know my surroundings. I explore the hotel and all its amenities. Everything is modern and lavish, from the gym and spa to the restaurants and bars. I meet Tiffany, who is on the main reception. She is very friendly and helpful. Everyone I have met, apart from Mr. Graham, has been lovely. I think I'm going to be very happy here.

In the evening Katie and I have a pizza delivered to my room and get to know each other more. I go to bed feeling really excited to start work tomorrow.

Chapter 4

Damien

After searching the hotel's staff database, I find Bella's records. The first moment I laid eyes on her, I knew I needed to find out everything about her. I feel drawn to her. I know I am stepping into dangerous territory, but I can't help myself. When I want something, I get it.

Bella is from a small town in the country and relocated recently. She is a hairdresser in the hotel's salon. She also lives in the staff quarters. It pleases me to know that she lives under my roof. Needing to see her again, I decide I could do with a haircut.

Foster & Thomas is a modern salon. It's spacious, black and white, clean, and professional looking. No expense was spared when kitting it out. I approach the receptionist and ask if anyone is free to cut my hair now. I just want a glimpse of Bella. I need my fix.

"I am very sorry, sir, but we are fully booked today," the receptionist tells me.

"Even for a quick trim?" I push.

I look around the busy salon as I am again refused, and to my disappointment, I don't see the golden- haired beauty I'm looking for. I am just about to leave when I hear the sweetest voice from across the room—Bella.

"Sarah, I think I can squeeze a gent's cut in. Mrs. Pye isn't quite ready to have her colour to be rinsed out yet, and if I get one of the assistants to shampoo for me, I can accommodate the gentleman." She walks over to the reception area and realises it is me.

"Damien, what a pleasant surprise," she says as her cheeks begin to flush with a rose pink that travels down to her chest.

"Bella, hello again. Thank you for fitting me in."

I love the way her body reacts to my presence.

"Would you like to follow me, sir?" Bella asks.

I do as she says. She seats me in a chair and places a gown around me. As she fastens the buttons around my neck, I can feel her fingers against my skin; they feel good. I start imagining what else those fingers could do.

Bella talks away while cutting my hair, she tells me how she has just moved to London and how much she is enjoying city life already. It's fascinating watching her work; she is such a perfectionist. The little faces she pulls as she concentrates have me smiling. Bella has just about finished styling my hair when she suddenly stiffens. The colour drains from her face, and the little smile she had just been wearing disappears.

I follow her gaze to see that smarmy arsehole who grabbed her the other night. He walks our way. Hold on a minute—I recognise the uniform he is wearing. He is a King employee? What? He can't be. Surely not! Fury builds inside me. Ripping the gown from around my neck, I force myself to stay calm and seated. My instinct is to smash the guy in the face and drag him outside by his ear—but him being an employee makes things difficult.

"Him!" I growl in fury.

Realising my fuse is about to blow, Bella puts a hand on my shoulder and whispers, "It's okay—I'll handle it. He's the hotel manager," she says.

Like hell he is. Not for much longer.

"There you are, Bella. I need to speak to you after work. You have some making up to do," he says, glaring at my Bella.

"LIKE HELL SHE DOES!" I shout, standing to face him. I have a least a foot in height on him. He's scared of me, I can tell, but he tries not to show it.

"Oh, It's you again. I should have you arrested for assault." He points his finger at me, and I lose my shit.

"I strongly recommend you walk out of here right now before you permanently lose the use of your legs!" I growl in the little man's face.

"Damien, please." Bella moves in between us,

putting her hand on my chest in a plea for me to calm down.

Strangely, her touch does exactly that.

The arsehole smirks nervously. "You obviously don't realise who you are talking to. I'll leave Bella to explain. Catch you later, Bella." He gives her a wink and walks out.

I want to kill him. Bella looks relieved when he leaves, but I can tell she is still worried about him.

I give Bella my business card and tell her "If he ever comes near you again, you must ring me that instant." I settle my bill and exit the salon.

The second I leave, I'm on the phone. "Penny, I need everything you can find on the Trinity manager down to his shoe size. Then contact him and tell him he has a meeting with the new CEO this evening. Oh, and get Mr. Davis here. I'm going to need his legal team to help me take this creep down."

"Consider it done Mr.King."

I end the call and ring Josh. "Josh, I need an additional security team at Trinity, and I want a guard on the door of the salon for the full opening hours. I also need you and Mr. Davis on a flight here now."

"Sure thing, Damien. I'll arrange the jet. You okay? You sound stressed." Josh always knows when there is more to things.

"I will be once I've eliminated a problem. I'm going to get Penny to send over some information on the soon-to-be-ex Trinity manager. I need you to dig deep—parking fines, previous employers, family, the lot. I need to know about it. This guy is going down, and I'm damn well going to make sure he doesn't take King along with him."

Bella

When Katie and I return to the salon after lunch, there is a security guard standing outside.

"Good afternoon, ladies. I'm Mike. I am the new Foster & Thomas security guard. I am here to keep you all safe. If you need anything at all, you just give me a shout," he announces.

"That's strange," says Katie. "We've never had security before. Maybe royalty or someone incredibly famous is coming?"

As we walk through the salon to get to the staffroom, we hear a commotion behind us at the salon entrance. Mr. Graham is trying to get inside. Mike is standing firmly in front of the doors, refusing to let him in.

"You cannot stop me going in there. I am the hotel manager! Whom do you report to? Give me their name. I will have your job!" Mr. Graham rages.

"I report to the 'King' himself, so you will have to take it up with him!" says Mike, standing strong, his arms folded in front of him.

Graham huffs, realising he isn't going to

win. He is about half the size of Mike—half as tall and half as wide. He gives Mike what he must think is a mean stare, then turns on his heel and leaves.

I have a feeling Damien is behind all this, but how? Then I remember him giving me his card. I'd just slipped it into my pocket and forgot about it. I pull it out and read the name on the card: *Damien King, CEO of King Security.*

Well, that explains where the security guard came from. I wonder if he is any relation to the Kings who own the hotel? Surely not. Just a coincidence, I'm assuming. I send him a quick text to thank him, put my phone in my bag, and continue with my busy day.

It turns out to be quite an eventful afternoon. Katie is shampooing her gentleman client when he starts making a suspicious movement under his gown. The area of the gown which lies over the groin area is bobbing up and down.

Being the confident little tigress that Katie is, she storms around to the front of the client and straight out demands, "What the hell do you think you are doing under there?"

Katie's raised voice attracts Mike's attention. He quickly intervenes and rips off the client's gown, revealing his hands. We had all assumed the worst, but he is, in fact, just cleaning his glasses.

That was an embarrassing situation for all. But the man left happily with a voucher for a year's worth of free haircuts as an apology.

After that, we have a client leave without paying. The lady, who is in her fifties, received a full colour change, Olaxplex treatments, and restyle haircut. The lady says she left her purse in her car. She leaves her handbag with her phone and belongings here while she nips to the car to get it. The bag is Gucci, and with the phone inside, it would definitely be worth more than the £300 bill. We expect her to be back within minutes. After an hour and a half, we realise she probably isn't coming back. On closer inspection of the handbag, it turns out to be a fake—and not a very good fake either, James informs us. There is also nothing in the bag apart from a few stones. We leave it with Mike to sort out.

At the end of the day, I check my phone I am excited to see a message waiting but am soon disappointed when I see it is from John.

John: Please can we talk face to face? X

Bella: I really don't think that's a good idea John. What is it you want to talk about?

As it is a nice day outside, I decide to go for a walk after work. When I get to the lobby, I see Tiffany in tears at the front desk.

"Hey, Tiffany. What's wrong?" I ask.

"It's Mr. Graham. He's just been down here shouting at everyone. Apparently, the new CEO of King is coming today and wants a meeting with Graham. He's not happy. He thinks someone has reported him for something. He said when he finds out who it is, he will make sure they never work again. I'm sure he thinks it's me, but it wasn't, I swear!" Tiffany looks really worried. Mr. Graham shouldn't be able to treat people like this.

"Well, if he hasn't done anything wrong, he has nothing to worry about," I say as I give Tiffany a hug.

I sit with her for a while and tell her all about my day—the incident with Graham, the poor man who was wrongly accused, and the lady with the fake bag. I think I have started to cheer her up.

"I can spot a fake Gucci a mile off," Tiffany chuckles. "I wish I worked in the salon. It sounds a lot more exciting than sitting at this desk all day."

A few minutes later, three men walk into the lobby, each of them wearing extremely expensive-looking suits that fit their muscular bodies perfectly. The first male is in his sixties, I'd say —a good-looking man for his age who obviously works out. The second man is in his thirties and is ruggedly handsome. He has a dangerous look in his eyes, as if he's seen a lot in his lifetime.

The third man takes my breath away.

Damien.

I thought a man couldn't be any sexier than the Damien I had already seen, but oh my God. Damien in a suit makes me burn with desire. His freshly cut dark hair is styled to perfection. He wears a black suit that clings to every broad curve of his body. Wow. I have never been jealous of an item of clothing before. His face bears a stern scowl. He is clearly a man on a mission.

As they walk past the desk, neither of them looking in our direction, I get a whiff of Damien's scent, so fresh and manly.

"Then again, sitting at this desk does have a few perks," Tiffany sighs, wide-eyed. She rests her chin in her hands, dreamily watching the three men disappear into the lifts. I experience strange a pang of jealousy I have no right to feel.

I text Katie to come down and meet us. The three of us decide to go and get some retail therapy. Just what we need after a day like today. The girls have great taste in clothes and a lot more style knowledge than me. With the help of Zara, John Lewis, and a few designer shops I have never heard of, I soon have a new wardrobe worthy of a London stylist.

We shop, drink cocktails, and laugh all evening. Katie is great; she is so confident, but in a lovely way. I really envy that about her. She doesn't care what anyone thinks of her and is happy in her own body as well as confident in her ability to do anything she puts her mind to. Tiffany is hilarious, especially after a couple of cocktails. She literally has no filter and has been telling Katie and me all about her latest sexual conquests.

"So, I was dating this guy—well, I had slept with him twice—and on our third date, he asked me to go to his place and he would cook me dinner. I was working that day, so I went straight there once I had finished. I had taken a change of clothes with me and asked if I could have a quick shower while he prepared the food. While I was in there washing, he came in to ask me how I liked my steak cooked. He liked what he saw, so I invited him in, obviously," she tells us with a twinkle in her eye. "We were really going for it, and I started to see stars. I thought, hey, this is good, no one's ever made me see stars before. But then my legs started to feel funny, and I realised I wasn't seeing stars—I was about to pass out. The thing was, I had been doing that intermittent fasting diet. I was fasting every day until one. But I had been so busy at work, it got to four o'clock before I realised I hadn't eaten. Then I thought, I don't want to spoil my dinner this evening, so I won't eat now. I guess my sugar level just dropped too low. I fainted in the shower midsex!" She bursts into laughter.

"Oh, my God, Tiffany—that could only happen to you!" Katie shrieks.

"That's not the worst bit. When I woke up on the bathroom floor—naked, I might add—I was looking at the face of a woman in her 60s. Turns out, he lived next door to his mum, and he had gone and got her to help me." Tiffany puts her face in her hands, and we all have a good laugh. "I got up, grabbed my clothes, and went home. Needless to say, I haven't seen him again."

The evening passes quickly and its almost midnight when we part ways.

When I get back to my room, I feel pretty great. I have really settled in and made some good friends. I put my new clothes away and get in the shower. My mind wanders to Damien and what he has been doing tonight. It obviously has something to do with Mr. Graham. I wonder if one of those guys he was with is the new CEO. I'm sure I'll find out soon enough.

Chapter 5

Damien

Mr. Graham, or David Graham Jones, as he is actually named, is about to go down. Penny has found numerous complaints and allegations of sexual harassment against Graham. Unfortunately, these allegations have never been taken any further. The employees who made the complaints left the company the day after the issues were raised. Graham being the manager, these complaints were hidden. When Josh delves further, he finds that Graham used a false name when applying for the role of hotel manager. David Graham Jones has a string of offences to his name, including sexual harassment and domestic violence.

I am sickened to think that this man has been walking around my father's hotel, wearing the King name on his chest. Not for much longer.

Mr. Davis, my solicitor, has gone through all the evidence and allegations both Josh and Penny found. We've contacted all the women involved and offered our deepest apologies as well as compensation and counselling for their ordeal.

Mr. Davis will ensure that the King name will not be tarnished by this disgusting man. He will also serve a considerable time in prison, providing the victims are willing to testify, but we will support them with this.

Ten minutes before our scheduled meeting, I walk into the hotel manager's office. Graham stands up.

"What are you doing here?! How dare you just walk into my office unannounced!" Graham shouts in his weaselly voice.

I repeat his own words back to him. "You obviously don't realise who you are talking to!"

The look on his face as the penny drops is priceless.

Mr. Davis and Joshua then enter the room. Mr. Davis and I take a seat. Josh stands by the door, wearing his "I can snap you in two with my bare hands" death scowl. I let Mr. Davis do all the talking. I just sit there and watch the colour drain from Graham's face. I watch him look around the room, planning his escape. But there is no way out for him other than the door that two police officers are standing behind. I enjoy watching him squirm as Mr. Davis reads out all the accusations and evidence we have on him. By the end of it, Graham looks like a scared little boy.

Once Graham is driven away in the police car, I go to the conference room. I have asked all the hotel staff to attend an emergency meeting. I arrange two of them so that the hotel can still operate. I want to introduce myself, explain what has just happened, and reassure them that this abhorrent behaviour will not be tolerated.

The room starts to fill with employees all chattering amongst themselves, clearly wondering what is going on. Most of them do a double-take when they see me onstage and fall into silence. Good. I may be a fair man, but I am their boss, and I will be respected. Bella enters with the second group. Our eyes meet immediately. Wearing all white, she looks like an angel. Her is hair damp and wavy, her face makeup free and flawless. She is the most beautiful woman in the room—in most rooms, probably. I want her. I need to be inside her tonight. I am going to wrap this up quickly and get her into my bed. She is just what I crave after the day I have had.

Bella

I get out of the shower, and there is a panicked banging on my door. I quickly open it, and Katie walks in.

"We need to go downstairs to the conference room immediately. Every hotel employee has been asked to attend a mandatory emergency meeting. Ours starts in five minutes. We need to hurry," she tells me in a panic.

I throw on a white T-shirt dress, quickly towel dry my hair, and head down with her.

"What do you think this is all about, Katie?"

I ask.

"Well, I've heard whispers that Graham was escorted out of the hotel by two police officers and that there is a new, very hot CEO," she gossips.

It wouldn't surprise me if Damien had something to do with all this.

As soon as we enter the conference room my suspicions are proved right. Damien stands on stage in front of half the hotel staff. Our eyes meet immediately. There is a hunger and desire within them that he bores into mine.

"Hey, Bella? Do you know him? He's looking right at you," Katie whispers to me.

"Erm, kind of" is all I can manage to get out.

I watch Damien as he confidently speaks to the room. He has a powerful and impressive presence.

"Good evening, everyone. I first would like to introduce myself. My name is Damien King. Sadly, due to the recent passing of my father, I am now the CEO of King Hotels."

There's a quiet sigh and a few soft words amongst the employees. It seems everyone thought very highly of the late Mr. King.

"It has always been paramount to my father that King employees are treated as family. Unfortunately, after noticing a high staff turnover in this hotel, it came to my attention that the man whom you have known as 'Mr. Graham' has been acting extremely inappropriately. I cannot go into too much detail, but I will say this. At King we will not tolerate this kind of behaviour. I am deeply sorry that this situation has happened in our hotel." Everyone in the room listens intently to his every word. He does genuinely seem deeply sorry.

"I have several people stationed around the room who all wearing red badges. They are part of our health and well-being team, they're here to help you. If you have had any inappropriate dealings with Mr. Graham, I urge you to speak to them once I have finished. We also have a new security team around the hotel who is here for your safety as well as that of our guests. Please confide in them if you need anything. They will put you in contact with the necessary team—all confidential, of course. There will be a new hotel manager here tomorrow, and I'm sure they will be of the highest standard. Thank you for taking the time to listen to me, and please remember that there are always people here who will listen to you. If you will now excuse me, I have some urgent business I need to take care of."

The room erupts in applause and chatter. Damien leaves the stage and comes straight towards me. "Miss White, I need you to come with me urgently."

Stunned, I look at Katie, whose eyes are wide open, her jaw almost on the floor.

"Okay," I say as he ushers me out of the room.

Out in the hallway, Damien grabs my hand,

sending shivers through my body. He obviously feels this, too, as he looks at me with a proud smile. He guides me through a door I hadn't even noticed before. In front of us is a lift that needs a code to access it. Damien enters it into the keypad, and the doors opens immediately.

"Where are we going?" I ask breathlessly.

Damien puts his hands around my waist, pulls me in to him, and whispers in my ear. "From the very first moment I saw you, I wanted to kiss you here." Damien kisses my neck below my ear, sending tingles down my body and covering my skin with goosebumps. "And here." He begins trailing kisses down my neck and onto my shoulder.

I am lost in ecstasy for a moment until my good sense brings me back to reality. I push him back slightly so I can look at him.

"I am not sure what you think is going to happen here, Damien, but I am not going into that lift with you. I have only met you a handful of times. I am really grateful you saved me from Graham that night; goodness knows what would have happened if you had not intervened. But I will not be abruptly taken from my friend and forcefully escorted to an unknown place. I may owe you one, but I will not be repaying you like this. You will have to think of another way," I say, folding my arms to try and make myself look more confident.

A small smirk of a smile curls one side of his

mouth, but it soon disappears into the stern, dark stare that he usually wears.

"You do not owe me anything, Bella. I thought this was something we both wanted," he says as he strokes the tip of his finger from my shoulder down my arm. Goosebumps follow his trail. "I guess I misread the signs. Please forgive me." He straightens himself and returns to his powerful demeanour as he enters the lift and immediately closes the doors behind him. I'm left staring at my reflection in the mirrored lift doors.

Have I just made the worst mistake of my life?

Damien

I am livid. Livid with myself. Why does this woman have such an effect on me? I lose control of my senses when I am around her. I feel extremely shaken by the experience. No woman has ever turned me down before. You think this would encourage me to move on, but it only makes my desire for her stronger. I have always acquired what I wanted in life. I work hard to ensure I get what I want, and this is no exception. I will have her—it may just take a little longer than I originally thought.

Unfortunately my Bella conquest needs to take a back seat for now, as tomorrow is my father's burial and private funeral. He is finally going to be laid to rest next to my mother. I'm feeling unnervingly emotional tonight. Bella has really got under my skin.

I have had enough of this day. I down a scotch and go to bed.

"Forever and ever. Amen," the vicar prays as he places my dad's ashes into the plot with my mum.

I am surrounded by family members and my father's closest associates. My mind, however, is a world away from here. It's a warm sunny day, not a cloud to be seen, and the sky is a vibrant shade of blue. It reminds me of Bella's eyes. I think back to last night, how she felt in my arms and her skin on my lips until she abruptly dismissed me. There's a pat on my back, and I realise the service is over. I'm standing alone next to my parents' memorial. To anyone else, I look like the grieving son; little do they know, my thoughts are with a beautiful blonde. I'm putting this unfamiliar obsession with Bella down to the emotional experiences I have been through during the last twelve months. Losing both parents in such a short space of time has had more of an effect on me than I thought. I turn to see George, who has also been a strong father figure in my life. I nod, and we leave to join the guests at the wake.

I do my rounds, speaking to everyone who has attended to pay their respects. I have always known what a kind and generous man my father was, but hearing stories about his life today has made me even more proud and ever more determined to ensure that his great legacy continues. I'm getting ready to leave when I hear a commotion outside. My blood boils as I see who is responsible. Pete.

"What the hell are you doing here?" I storm at Pete, but Josh steps in between us. On any other day I'd have more time for him, but not today. I've tried many times to apologise to Pete but it just makes him worse. He knows the guilt I feel for what happened his sister, but he continues to provoke me.

Pete is clearly drunk. He looks angry and upset.

"I came here hoping to see you in pain from having lost a loved one. I hoped you might now feel the suffering you have inflicted on my family. Only now that I'm here, I remember what a cold, heartless man you are. Your father was a great man, but you.... He must have been so disappointed," he says bitterly.

"Get him out of here!" I shout "Before I do something I'll regret." Two of my security team grab him by the arms and carry him down the path. His legs scramble to keep up with their pace.

"I'll get you one day, Damien!" he shouts back at me.

I laugh at his statement. This guy has a death wish.

Bella

Weeks go by, and I hardly see Damien again properly. I have seen him now and again, walking through the hotel or speaking with employees. I secretly observe him from a distance. He hasn't once looked at me or tried to contact me. I assume he has given up on me, since I rejected him that day by the lift. I hoped not, though; I miss him, strangely. I've started to regret turning him down that day. Every night, I lie in bed, imagining what might have happened, what it would have felt like. I am starting to drive myself mad with the obsession.

I throw myself into work to take my mind off him. After all, that was why I came to London —to concentrate on my career. Thankfully we have a big event coming up in a couple of months. An exclusive hair and beauty event. It's the perfect thing to take my mind off Damien. The Foster & Thomas team are doing the hair of six models. We are teaming up with fashion stylists and makeup artists to create a unique but on-trend look to help promote a new sustainable and eco-friendly hair products and tools company. The event is being held in the Trinity Hotel. It is an invitation-only event, so only the best in the industry will be there. It is to be an evening of gourmet food and fancy cocktails with an entertaining exhibition showcasing the latest eco-friendly products, fashion, makeup and hair designs. It is going to be spectacular. There is a whole production team organising it.

The models will be doing a dance routine. There will be music, lights, and even fireworks. I am very excited. First, the models are doing a routine in casual clothes, then while the guests are eating, we will be backstage transforming them into glamourous looks fit for a ball. Once finished, the models will do another routine, which is much more upbeat with fancy lights and little sparkling fireworks. At the end, one of our stylists is to present the work we have done and talk all about the wonderful products and tools we used. The whole team and I assumed that Rebecca would take the lead on this, as she is the manager and franchise owner. However, the eco brand has asked me to be the one to present.

Apparently, they feel I am more passionate about their ethos. I am not sure Rebecca is thrilled with this, but she doesn't say anything other than that as long as the brand is happy, so is she. When I was first asked, I almost said no. I panicked. I am still panicking now, but this is the whole reason I moved to London—for opportunities like this. I need to do it. The clothes stylists and makeup artists are brilliant. We all get on really well together, bouncing ideas off one another, all really motivated, and we come up with some amazing results.

It's a Thursday evening, after the salon has closed, everyone involved meets in the King Suite to discuss plans for the event. This is where the event is being held. The King Suite is the biggest, most spectacular room in the hotel. It's used for weddings and other very special events. I dread to think how much it would cost to hire this room for a day.

The space takes your breath away when you enter. The floor is a white-and-grey marble that glitters ever so slightly. One wall has six floor-to-ceiling arched windows, revealing the most beautiful view of Trinity Square Gardens. Three modern crystal chandeliers hang from the ceiling. The crystals appear to float in midair; they sparkle immensely and project tiny rainbows across the vaulted ceiling.

The events team is setting up a stage with a runway down the centre of the room. I start to feel ripples of nerves and excitement. While looking around the room, taking it all in, to my left, I catch sight of captivating eyes upon me. There he is. Damien. As handsome and as dreamy as ever. My heart skips a beat and begins to flutter in my chest. What is it about him? His dark hair—which is looking ready for a trim, actually—his strong jaw and cheekbones covered with a little more stubble than I'd seen him with before. The usual scowl on his face. The twinkle in his eye. Damn, when he looks at me, it is like we are the only two people in the room. He is wearing all black. Tight jeans and a long-sleeve T-shirt. He gets sexier every single time I see him. He literally takes my breath away.

My legs buckle slightly as his eyes run down

my body. To hide my stumble and jelly legs, I walk around the room. Damien is with four other men, who are all also wearing black; they have King Security jumpers on. They must be planning the security for the event. Forcing myself to look away in order to pull it together, I try and focus on the reason why I am here, which is to work. But as I look at the other women in the room, I see that most have their eyes turned in Damien's direction. They look at him admiringly and flirtatiously, and I can't help but feel jealous! Their gazes start to move, and they begin to chatter. I then realise this is because Damien is on the move—he is heading towards me. I feel a little smug.

"Bella, I was hoping to see you tonight."

His deep masculine voice vibrates in my every nerve. In my head I do an excited dance —maybe I will get a second chance. I have been kicking myself ever since I turned him down.

"You were? And why is that?" I ask, trying to remain calm and not give away the excitement burning inside me.

"Yes—my hair is ready for trim, I wondered if you would be able to fit me in before Monday? I have a meeting I need to look my best for."

My heart sinks a little. He just wants his hair cut.

"I can check the diary tomorrow, but I'm sure I'm fully booked for the next couple of weeks, unfortunately," I reply, actually disappointed. I really want to see him, so I decide to not waste this opportunity. "I do feel as though I owe you a favour, though." I continue, "so, I'd be happy to do it tomorrow night when I finish work or over the weekend?"

I then realise that tomorrow is Friday, and he most definitely will have plans, and I have blatantly just told him I literally have no plans. What a loser. I do regret turning him down, but I don't want to appear desperate.

"You owe me nothing, Bella. But tomorrow night will work for me. If you don't mind working out of hours. What time do you finish at the salon?"

"I finish around six.," I say, hoping I'll have time to change and refresh before seeing him. A Friday is a long, busy day in the salon, I definitely will not be looking or smelling my best when I finish.

"Seven o'clock tomorrow night, then. I will text you the details," he replies, then turns and walks back towards the security team. No small talk, just matter-of-fact, and gone.

It takes me a couple of minutes to register what just happened and catch my breath. I take my phone out of my bag and open my calendar. I add an entry for tomorrow evening that reads "Damien, haircut." Not that I will forget, but I just need a small task to complete while my heart rate returns to normal.

I just about manage to compose myself while the events team runs through the order of the evening. We discuss our ideas for lighting and music to go with our themes. Everyone is really excited, and the energy is infectious. It is going to be a great night, and I am feeling more confident. I just wish I had as much faith in myself as everyone else has. Everyone seems to value my opinion on everything.

As soon as I leave the room, thoughts of Damien return to me. Does he just want me to cut his hair? Surely he could get his hair cut anywhere with the click of his fingers. Maybe he just likes the way I cut it? Or maybe this is an excuse for something more. I am hoping for the latter.

I wake early the next morning to prepare for my appointment with Damien in the evening. I won't be wasting this opportunity. He hasn't messaged me the details yet, but I know I have to be ready for 7:00, which doesn't leave me much time after work. I shower before my shift and make sure I am silky smooth and hair free—you know, just in case. I wash and dry my hair, styling it in curls so I can brush them out later for a loose, natural wave. I don't want to look like I'm trying too hard, but I want to look good.

I iron my outfit and leave it hanging up, ready to put on when I return. I decide on a light blue denim dress. The colour looks good with my blonde hair and blue eyes. It is casual but shows some leg, so it's a little sexy without looking like I am trying to be. I have some new nude wedges that will look great with it too. I arrive at the salon early so I can go on the sunbed before I start. All I need to do when I finish work is to have a quick shower, get changed, brush my hair, and apply a little make up.

I check my phone as I get off the sunbed.

Damien: Meet me in the lobby at 7pm. Make sure you're hungry. I'll order in.

He is so demanding. No pleasantries—so hot! My stomach flutters with butterflies as I think about this evening. I have a feeling today is going to be a long day of clock watching, and it is.

Chapter 6

Damien

It has been a couple of weeks since I made a fool of myself with Bella. I stupidly assumed she is the same as the many other women I've "dated." That she would fall into bed with me as soon as I asked. I have known from the first moment I saw her that she is different. There is no comparison. Yes, all women I have been with before were very beautiful. They have the figure, the face, the hair, the tits—mostly fake. But Bella's figure is a perfect hourglass and all natural. Her face has flawless skin that flushes, moves, and wrinkles up with her expressions and emotions. Most of the women I date have had that much Botox, I cannot tell when they are happy or sad. Her eyes sparkle; they are captivating. They remind me of the sea. Her beauty shines from the inside, and I need to have some of that.

After she turned me down a few weeks ago, I tried to stay away. I now know that Bella isn't the sort of woman who would just have a one-night stand. Although I am not sure one night would be enough with Bella anyway. Hopefully a few nights with Bella will get her out of my system, and I will be able to move forward. I think about her too often, and although I've tried to satisfy my needs elsewhere, no one can even come close to taking the edge off the desire I feel for Bella. I need her. Once I have her, I'm hoping this unusual obsession will subside. Not being in control of my feelings unnerves me.

I knew I would bump into her at the event planning last night. I used the excuse of my hair needing a cut, but I worried that would only get me minutes with her in the salon. When she offered to do it out of work hours, she gave me the opportunity I've been hoping for. This is my chance to change her opinion of me. I want to wine and dine her, show her how much of a gentleman I can be. I may not want to have a relationship with Bella, but I still want to treat her well and give her a little pleasure. This is my opportunity, and I'm going to use it to my full advantage.

The view from my penthouse suite is spectacular. The timing is perfect, as we will be able to watch the sunset while we dine. I ask Penny to order everything from the menu of the hotel's fine-dining restaurant, since I'm not sure what she likes. It will be set out on the dining table in front of the floor—to-ceiling windows. I think about buying Bella a gift, but I feel that would be too much for her. After all, she thinks she is just coming to cut my hair and have a bite to eat. I don't want to scare her off again.

I've had a busy day working through hotel stuff and business planning with Josh, but that hasn't stopped me from checking the time every half hour and thinking about the promising evening ahead with Bella.

"What's with you lately?" asks Josh. "You're always deep in thought. If you need some time off, mate, I can manage security, and the new hotel manager seems like she knows what she's doing. Why don't you take a break—it's not been long since your father passed. You need to grieve."

I look at Josh, registering what he has just said. "No! I'm needed here."

Josh stares at me, not believing a word. "Okay, well, I have left the CVs and profiles of the new recruits on your desk. Do you want to look at them before I do their final interviews?" he asks.

"I'll have a look later. You know what you're doing. I trust your judgement," I reply as I leave the room.

The truth is, yes—I am grieving for my father, but the real issue on my mind is Bella. I have no idea what my head and emotions are doing; it's all very new and confusing to me, but I need to find out what is going on. I need to be here at the hotel, near Bella.

Seven o'clock arrives, and I'm in the lobby, waiting for Bella. One of the security team approaches me with a question. While he's talking to me, Bella enters the lobby. She looks like an angel—her golden blonde hair fanned out in waves, her pretty little face with those captivating blue eyes. She is wearing a denim dress that hugs those beautiful curves. Her long, toned legs are mesmerising, I can't wait to have them wrapped around me. It's like the world stands still as she walks in slow motion towards me. The sun shines through the doors, lighting up a halo around her. I have to have her. She is meant for me. She will be mine.

I dismiss my employee. I don't care if I am rude. I need to get to Bella.

"Good evening, Bella. May I take your case?" I ask as she pulls a little black case behind her, which I assume contains the things she needs to cut my hair.

"Good evening to you, too, Damien. Yes, thank you—that's very kind," she says as she motions for me to take the case.

I excitedly usher her towards the penthouse lift.

"I want to apologise again for the last time we stood here," I say as I type in the code for the lift. "You do not deserve to be treated like that. I hope we can start again?"

"All is forgiven. Don't say another word about it," she replies with a coy smile.

"Thank you," I reply, instantly relieved.

When we enter the lift Bella stumbles a little. Instantly I catch hold of her arm to steady her. She giggles in embarrassment. I'm filled with anticipation by the closeness of our bodies in such a confined space.

The lift doors open into the hallway of the penthouse, and I guide Bella into the kitchen. I sense she is a little nervous, so I offer her a drink.

"I have wine? Beer? Spirits? Anything you like, really—there's a full bar in the dining room," I say.

"Wine would be lovely, thank you, but just a small glass. I haven't eaten since lunch, and I need to keep a steady hand while cutting your hair, or you may lose an ear," she chuckles nervously.

The sound makes my cock stir.

"Very well. I have a nice bottle of red I've been wanting to open. Would you like to eat first?" I ask. "I ordered the menu from the restaurant. It is being set out as we speak. It should only be a few more minutes."

"That's sounds lovely, but would it be okay if I did your hair first so that I can relax? It's been a long, busy week, and food and wine sound like just what I need," Bella replies with the most beautiful smile.

I love it when she smiles. I want to put that smile on her lips all the time, amongst other things.

"You get your things set up, then, and I'll go and check on the food."

I enter the dining room and even I'm impressed. The food is displayed expertly. There are flower arrangements on the table and dotted around the room. Candles are flickering, giving the room a cosy and romantic feel. With the skyline backdrop visible through the window, it is pretty incredible. I feel like I have forgotten something, though. Is something missing? I can't think what, so I put it down to my paranoid subconscious.

"You have outdone yourself yet again," I say to Penny as she stands there proudly.

"Thank you, Mr. King. I am glad it is to your satisfaction. Now, is there anything else you need for this evening?" she asks.

"No, thank you, Penny. That will be all for tonight," I say with a nod.

"Okay, dear. Good luck! Just be yourself." Penny gives me a warm smile that I return with a frown.

Penny, like George, is family to me. They are both very professional towards me, but sometimes they show their feelings. This is the first time she has commented on an encounter with a lady friend, though; does she know something I don't? I just hope Bella likes it.

I return to the kitchen, and Bella is all set up. I take a seat in the bar stool she has lowered and let her work her magic. Bella chatters away while she works, and her voice instantly relaxes me. She's so close, I just want to reach out and touch her, but I don't. Her scent does things to my body. My skin tingles in response to her fingers moving through my hair and touching my ears. Once she's finished, she stands in front of me to "check the balance, as she has no mirror"—or that is her excuse, anyway.

I open my legs wider so she can get closer, and she bends slightly so we are eye to eye. I can feel her breath on my face, I'm fighting so hard not to reach out and pull her those extra few inches.

Once she's finished, I help Bella clear up and pack away her things. She is still chatting away, telling me all about her day and the eccentric clients she's had this week. She's so expressive when she speaks. Her stories could be the most boring in the world, but told by Bella, you are enthralled by every word.

I invite Bella into the dining room. "Dinner is served, would you like to follow me." I enter first, so I can see her expression as she walks in. She doesn't disappoint. I knew she would appreciate this. Other women I have dated wouldn't have batted an eyelid, but Bella values things, and I love that about her.

"Oh my, Damien—this is beautiful. Do you have guests coming?" she exclaims.

"Only you," I reply.

"There's so much food. This can't possibly be for just us?"

Bella looks panicked. I hope this hasn't backfired. I just want her to relax and enjoy the evening.

"I wasn't sure what your tastes were, so I've ordered one of everything off the menu. But don't worry, once we've finished, I'll have the rest sent down to the security team room. They'll be happy to finish the rest, I'm sure." Bella seems to relax a little. "Now what do you fancy, Bella?" Me, I hope.

Bella chooses the sea scallops to start and a seafood pasta for her main course. We sit facing each other, and I more than enjoy the view. Bella is really relishing her food; her expressions and the little appreciative noises she makes have me painfully aroused. I like the fact she feels comfortable enough to eat in front of me. Most women I've dated order tiny salads and push them around their plate.

"So, why have you moved to London?" I ask her.

Bella's face lights up as she speaks about hairdressing. You can tell it isn't just a job to her—it's her passion. She explains how where she used to live, there weren't many opportunities for her to advance in her career, and her dream was to work in the fashion industry. Bella describes her hometown and how different it is there compared to the fast pace of London city. She talks of her parents and friends she left behind, but I get the feeling she is leaving something out.

"Any boyfriends I should know about?" I ask.

As soon as the words leave my mouth, Bella's head sinks slightly. She looks down at her food, and her beautiful smile and the sparkle in her eye are replaced with a sad, hurt expression. The sight of this makes my blood boil, and I instantly want to hurt the person who put that look on her face.

"No boyfriend," she says. "Just a crazy ex,

but that's a story for another day." She forces a laugh.

I don't push any more than that because I want to see the return of her smile. I will be getting to the bottom of that hurt expression, though, and do my best to eradicate the reason. Crazy ex—I will find out about him.

We finish our dinner, and I want to be closer to Bella. The table between us suddenly feels extremely large and obstructive.

"Shall we go into the sitting room?" I ask hopefully.

Chapter 7

Bella

"Are you sure I'm not keeping you from something, Damien?" I ask as we enter the sitting room.

Damien's apartment is magnificent. I have never seen anything like it. I am overwhelmed with the whole situation. The dining room, the décor, the flowers, the candles, all that delicious food—I can't quite believe he has done all that for me. I am sure he has been expecting guests who have cancelled at the last minute. Surely he wouldn't have gone to all that trouble and expense for me?

When Damien said he would arrange some food for the evening, as I was cutting his hair, I assumed it would be a takeout pizza or similar and then maybe a drink or two. I thought I would have to do a little flirting to let him know I was still interested, since I wasn't sure if he still was. But maybe he is. He seems to be making a lot of effort.

"All you are keeping me from is a lonely night in front of the telly. I am really enjoying your company, Bella."

The way Damien says my name sends prickles down my back and flutters in my stomach. He opens another bottle of wine and fills up my glass.

A lady called Penny and a man called George come into the apartment and take all the food down to the security team. I am glad it isn't going to waste, as we hardly made a dint in the spread, even though I am feeling rather stuffed. Penny and George are a really friendly couple. They speak perfect Queen's English, and although they obviously work for Damien, I can tell they think a lot of him.

I'm starting to feel a little tipsy. We have talked, laughed, and flirted for what feels like hours. I decide I have had enough wine for the evening and ask for some water. I follow Damien into the kitchen. He gets me a bottle from the fridge and pours it into a glass. I watch his every move. How does he make pouring a drink so sexy, so seductive? As Damien hands me the glass, he puts his arm around my waist and pulls me towards him.

He lightly touches my cheek and tucks some loose hair behind my ear. He stares into my eyes. "Bella, you really are the true meaning of the word."

His gaze drops to my lips, and before I know it, his firm but ever so soft lips are on mine. He pushes my lips open with his, and we begin to explore each other's mouths with our tongues.

Damien kisses me with so much passion. I have never felt aroused from kissing, but this is a whole new experience. My knees begin to buckle, and he takes my weight. With one effortless sweep, he lifts me and sets me on the kitchen island. The cold of the marble on the backs of my thighs and bum just add to the sensations going on between my legs. Damien nudges my knees open with his hips and stands in between my thighs. With me sitting on the island, our eyes are now level.

Damien cups my face in his hands and looks deep into my eyes as he says, "From the very first moment I laid eyes on you, Bella, I wanted to kiss you." He begins kissing my cheek, moving towards my ear. "To touch you."

His kisses a trail down my neck. My back arches at the tingles he sends down my body. He holds the base of my head in one of his hands and gently massages the nape of my neck. He massages my thigh with his other hand, moving upwards towards the heat that throbs in between them. I let out an uncontrollable gasp as he reaches my swollen sex that has now made my thong damp. Damien's mouth moves back to mine, and he gives me the deepest, hungriest kiss I have ever experienced.

"Lie back. Let me take care of you," he instructs.

His voice is firm and commanding. I like it. I do as he asks. He pulls my thong to the side, and his lips are suddenly on my aching, sensitive spot.

I jump a little at the sensation; this isn't something I am used to, but I have a feeling I'm going to enjoy it.

Damien works on my clit with his tongue, round and round, up and down with the perfect amount of pressure. He then enters me with his fingers, curling them, searching to find that bundle of nerves and gosh does he find it! Stroking and rubbing, he works his hands and his mouth methodically together. The feeling is something I have never experienced before. The heat and desire are overwhelming, and I am soon seeing stars.

"Oh my God, Damien!" I gasp, my back arching. He continues until my orgasm subsides. I pull him up to meet my lips. I can taste myself on his lips, and it is the hottest thing I have ever experienced in my life. Damien King has just ruined me for all other men.

Damien sits me up, and we just hold each other until our breathing returns to a normal pace. I look into Damien eyes, cupping his jaw, pressing my forehead against his. With anyone else, I would feel very self-conscious after what we just did, but Damien makes me feel comfortable and safe.

"I need you in my bed!" he says in a firm, deep, rough voice.

He looks at me, clearly waiting for my consent. I nod. Damien effortlessly picks me up in his big strong arms. He walks me through the penthouse and into his bedroom. The lights come on as soon as we enter the room.

"Lights on. Blinds closed," Damien instructs.

The lights dim, and the blinds on the floor-to-ceiling windows close. If I wasn't so mesmerised by Damien, I would be crushing over this room with its fancy gadgets. Damien gently but forcefully throws me on to the bed. He stares at me with his smouldering eyes, which are dark and dominating. I would literally do anything he asks of me at this minute. He runs his eyes all over my body, looking like a predator about to devour his prey.

When Damien begins unbuttoning his shirt, all I can do is stare. I burn with desire. His shirt parts to reveal his glistening olive skin, his broad shoulders, and perfectly formed muscular chest. Am I in some kind of dream about a Greek god? My mouth waters at the thought of running my tongue over his skin and sucking on his nipples. What has come over me? I've never had thoughts like this before, and the things I feel, I didn't even know were possible. I must let out a gasp or whimper, as Damien comes over to me and pulls me towards him.

He cups my face and looks into my eyes. "Are you okay, Bella?" he asks.

Oh Christ—the way he says my name.

"Yes." I say in a gasp. He literally takes my breath away.

"Good. If you want me to stop at any point, you tell me. You can leave at any time, Bella. But believe me, I will never hurt you. I just want to pleasure you and for you to see how beautiful you are to me."

His words have me dizzy. My head nods eagerly. My body desperate for more.

He kisses me on the forehead and steps back. "Now take off your dress."

I kneel on the bed and unfasten all my buttons. I let my dress fall to the covers. Damien's eyes are on my breasts. His breathing is faster, and I can see his pulse racing in his neck. I unhook my bra and let it fall as well. Damien's Adam's apple moves up and down as he gulps. The bulge in his trousers looks painful. I feel elated that I am the one who is making his body react this way.

"Come here, Damien," I say, and he steps towards me.

We kiss like our lives depend on it. While we devour each other, I reach down and open his button and zip. Damien helps me remove his pants, and I am greeted with the most glorious sight that makes my sex heat up and my cheeks flush. It is so smooth and perfectly shaped, the end glistening with his excitement. The main thing I notice is the size. Damien is big. Bigger than I've even seen, anyway; well, I suppose I've only ever seen John's, so I don't really have much to compare it to.

"Don't worry, I won't hurt you," Damien says.

He must have seen me staring and read my mind. He picks me up and lays me on the bed.

"Lie on your front," he commands.

I obey and rest my head in my folded arms.

Damien whispers into my ear, "I want to kiss and taste every part of your body. You are so beautiful, Bella."

"Hmmm." I'm in heaven.

He lifts my hair and kisses the back of my neck; goose bumps tingle all the way down my body. He spreads my legs and kneels in between them. Damien massages and kisses every part of me, starting at my neck and shoulders, down each arm, up and down my back, my bottom, each leg, and my feet. If I wasn't so aroused, I could have fallen asleep. Every kiss and squeeze of his hands makes me warmer and wetter. He caresses my bottom, and I can't take any more. I need to touch him. I need him inside me. I flip myself over and pull him down onto me. I grab Damien's head and pull him to my lips.

He reaches down between my legs. "You're ready for me," he says with a sparkle in his eyes.

He reaches into the drawer at the side of the bed and pulls out a condom. He sits up and rolls it on. I watch and feel the heat rise inside me. He nestles himself into my opening and slowly enters me. Damien lets out a satisfied groan. The stretching and filling sensation is incredible. Once he is fully inside me, I cry out in pleasure.

Damien looks me in the eyes. "Are you okay, Bella?" he asks.

I could orgasm right then, but I hold back.

"Perfect," I reply.

At that assurance, Damien begins to thrust in and out, maintaining our eye contact as he does. He lifts my legs to get himself deeper. The pressure is intense, but it's just what I need. We soon move in unison, caressing each other with our hands and mouths. I can't get enough of him.

"I've been thinking about this since the first time I saw you," he pants.

"Oh fuck, I feel exactly the same way." I admit.

"I can't hold out much longer—come with me Bella!"

I don't need much persuasion. I am already there. Stars appear in my eyes, and my sex tightens around Damien's.

"Aaarrgghh Fuck! Bella!" Damien groans and pounds harder as we both reach our climax.

With one last push, he shudders; then he holds me like he never wants to let me go. I wrap my legs around him, and we lie there catching our breaths and enjoying the aftermath of our pleasure. Our sweat-glistening bodies fit together like they were made for each other.

"That was incredible," Damien sighs as he eventually releases me and heads to what I assumed is the ensuite.

He comes back in a moment, having discarded the condom, climbs back into bed, and wraps his arms around me.

"Will you stay here with me tonight?" he

asks.

This is not how I saw tonight going, but I am feeling a little tipsy and absolutely exhausted after my two orgasms, and I just am not ready to leave him yet.

"Okay," I reply snuggling into him. I haven't known Damien for very long, but this just feels familiar, safe, and right.

We don't say anything more to each other, both obviously feeling comfortable in each other's arms. We drift into a deep sleep, our bodies entwined.

Chapter 8

Bella

I wake up feeling like I slept well. Even after the wine I drank last night, I feel refreshed and fulfilled. I smile to myself, remembering the night's events and Damien's hands all over my body as he pleasured every part of me. I felt worshiped and adored. Buzzing noises to my right make me open my eyes fully, and I stretch out. I realise I am in bed alone.

I look at the bedside table to see my phone flashing and vibrating. I pick it up to see that it's Katie. She has rung me three times and sent me four messages. Her latest one reads:

Katie: I know you didn't come home last night. You're either in a ditch somewhere or you got lucky. If I don't hear from you in 5 minutes, I'm starting a search party!

Bella: I'm so sorry Katie. I should have let you know. I'm fine. I'll catch up with you soon xx

Katie: Thank God! I've been so worried. Ok can't wait to hear where the hell you've been! Xx

It's 7:00 a.m., and I need to be at work in two hours. I put my phone back down and see a note that reads: *I'm in the kitchen. There's a robe on the chair.* I look around and see a black armchair with a fluffy white robe draped over it. I put it on and make my way to the kitchen. I can't quite remember the way, but I follow the smell of cooking bacon. The penthouse is huge; its white-and-grey marble floors are warm under my feet. I walk past the living room and into the kitchen.

There, with his back to me, stands Damien at the kitchen island. He is wearing grey lounge pants that cling to his bottom. His broad athletic shoulders tense as he cooks. Music is playing quietly in the background, and he dances slightly to the beat. I stand there for a moment, just taking in the view; surely this is a dream?

As if he can feel me watching him, Damien turns. His eyes land on me, making me melt. I feel a big smile spread across my face. What is it about him?

"You're up. I've made breakfast. I don't know about you, but after our workout last night, I'm rather hungry," he says with a grin.

I blush. "I'm a little hungry too."

We sit at the island. There are eggs, bacon, sausages—you name it, it's here. I hope he doesn't expect me to eat all this.

As if he can read my mind, he says, "I wasn't sure what you would prefer."

"This is amazing, Damien—thank you. Did you do all this yourself?" I ask.

He shrugs. "I did."

We chat while eating. I tell Damien my best friend Chloe from home is coming today and that I'm meeting her at the tube station after work. She is staying with me until Monday. Today is Saturday —she and I are having a girls' night tonight with dancing and cocktails. Then tomorrow we are going on an open-top bus tour around London to see the sights. I am so excited. It feels such a long time since I have seen Chloe. I really have missed her. I can't wait to spend the weekend with her and tell her all my news.

Damien offers the use of his limousine for the weekend, but I tell him that won't be necessary. He is very persuasive, so I accept a lift to the open-top bus tour on Sunday. We would have had to get a taxi to the pick-up point anyway. Chloe will be extremely excited with a limo ride, so I am happy to accept his offer for that. I am planning on staying fairly local for drinks tonight. I still don't really know my way around yet, and the bars near the hotel are good—plus I just want to spend time with Chloe.

After breakfast, I get dressed and leave. Damien offers me the use of his shower, but I just want the comfort of my own bathroom. I need to gather my thoughts before work. I feel so overwhelmed with the amazing experience I've had this past twelve hours. I need some time to compose myself.

Damien

Back in my bedroom, I stare at my bed, reminiscing about my night with Bella. It was every bit as incredible as I had imagined, if not more so. I had thought, however, that after our love-making session, I would be able to shake off this infatuation or whatever it is I have for her. Unfortunately, those feelings seem to be even stronger today. Now I KNOW how good she feels, and I need more. What the hell is happening to me? Bella spent the night. I have never asked a woman to spend the night with me before. I usually can't wait for them to leave.

There's just something about Bella—*my* Bella. I wonder whether she feels the same about me? I hope not. It's too dangerous for her to have feelings for me. I must make sure things don't go too far. I have time yet, though, I'm sure. I'll make the most of being with Bella while I can.

My phone buzzes, snapping me out of my daydream.

"Josh. Safe flight? George should be waiting for you. Has he arrived?"

"Yeah, I'm here in one piece, and I can see George. I just wanted to check the plans for tonight," Josh replies, as tonight is a King Security team member's birthday.

"Just staying local. Some of the team are on jobs tomorrow, so it won't be a late one," I say.

Joshua has come back over again from New York to look into some possible premises and meet with a new client. It's starting to look like my stay in London will be longer than I had originally planned. I was supposed to be here for two weeks, but after the incident with the arsehole Graham, I need to make sure the hotel is running smoothly with the new manager. Then there is also Bella. London is my home, after all, and even though it has a lot of bad memories for me, it still feels good to be back. I wonder if I will bump into Bella tonight. Who am I kidding? Of course I will—I'll make sure of it.

"So, tell me about her," Josh demands as we stand at the hotel bar, drinking beer.

Josh doesn't beat around the bush; if he has something to say, he will come out and say it. He also reads people very well. Especially me.

"There's not much to tell. We fucked. That's it." I try to believe the words I say.

"That's definitely not 'it.' I can tell. You like her."

"What if I do? Nothing can come of it so that's that," I protest.

"Not all women are like…. *her*, you know. You don't need to keep punishing yourself."

"It wasn't *her* though was it. It was me. She did what she did because of the way I am. It's safer this way, Josh. I no longer want to discuss it."

Josh nods, and we talk about work. Josh knows when not to push me. He is wrong—I can't let anything serious happen between me and Bella.

I don't want to be responsible for something like that happening again.

We have a good evening. I have a couple of beers and a scotch, but that is about my limit unless I'm at home. I like to keep my wits about me while I'm out. We stay at the local bars, and I spot Bella in couple of them. I just admire her from a distance. She looks like she is having a good time with her friend Chloe. They are laughing and smiling, hugging and dancing. I like to see her happy. I don't want to intrude on their time or seem too eager, so I observe from afar.

We finish up at the hotel bar, which is more of a club at this time of night. It is dark, but I can still see my Bella. She is on the dance floor with Chloe. She looks incredibly sexy. Other men in the room have started to notice her, and it makes me angry. I don't want anyone else to look at her, or touch her, or even see that beautiful body. I have never been a jealous man, but this woman—I crave for her to be only mine.

Bella and her friend seem a little drunk now. They are still aware of what is going on, but I feel I should watch out for them just in case. Most of the security guys have left now. I suppose it's not much fun being out with your bosses when you have work the day after. It is just Josh and me at the bar.

"So that's her, is it?" He had followed my gaze. "She's hot."

"I know," I grumble as I bore holes with

my eyes into the heads of the men that have just surrounded Bella.

She seems oblivious to them, as she is having too much fun dancing and laughing with her friend. Her body moves so sexily but innocently. It is the fact that she doesn't realise how beautiful she is that makes her all the more attractive. One of the guys tries his luck, but Bella just waves him away. Good. Realising they have been surrounded, the girls move to the other side of the dance floor. But the dumbass obviously can't take no for answer. He grabs Bella from behind, wrapping his arm around her waist and starts to grind into her.

I see red. How dare he touch my Bella. I am over there before I know it. I grab him by the scruff of his neck and throw him to the floor. He gets up, but with one fist to the face, he is out for the night.

I turn to Bella, who looks rather shocked. "Are you okay?"

She nods and wraps her arms around herself. The dumbass's friends surround us, shouting for security, who immediately join us.

"This man just attacked our mate!" yells one of them rather drunkenly.

"We saw your mate. He has had far too much to drink, he's assaulted a lady, and then tripped and hit his face on the floor. You all need to leave now!" says the bar's security manager who just happens to be King Security.

The idiots do at least have some common

sense, as they leave without further argument. Chloe has her arm around Bella and watches me suspiciously.

"Are you sure you're okay? Did he hurt you?" I ask, still concerned.

"I'm fine, honestly. Thank you for getting rid of him," she says.

"Yeah, you saved me from having to break a few nails. I'm Chloe, by the way." Chloe holds out her hand.

"It's a pleasure to meet you Chloe. I'm Damien."

Chloe smiles at me as if she knows exactly who I am.

"Can I get you ladies a drink?"

The girls follow us back to the bar. Josh has been right behind me, just in case I needed back up. Josh always has my back, and vice versa.

The four of us talk well until the early hours. Chloe and Josh seem to get on well too. Josh deserves to meet someone nice. Chloe is an attractive girl—pretty face, darker hair than Bella, and has more of an athletic figure. She isn't as attractive as Bella—not in my eyes, anyway—but I can see what Josh would see in her. We say our good nights and go our separate ways. I want to invite Bella back to my place, but I know Chloe is staying with her, so it isn't an option. Another night, soon, I tell myself.

Chapter 9

Bella

"Oh my God, Bella—you said Damien was hot, but he is off the scale!" Chloe says as we stumble into my room. "And he's your knight in shining armour. Did you see how he just threw that guy to the ground and then punched him as if he weighed nothing? He's like Superman or the Hulk or something!"

I laugh—we are so drunk. I had such a good night with my best friend. I've missed her so much. We'd danced and laughed all night long.

"It's not the first time he's saved me from a drunk guy who got too handsy. Remember I told you about that night Graham had cornered me and then a guy stepped in and got rid of him? Well, that was Damien too!" I tell Chloe.

"Seriously, Bella, Damien has been sent to you from Cupid, or God, or karma or whoever it is that sends people. It all makes sense—he is your prince," Chloe says, slurring whilst trying to undress.

"I'm not sure about that, Chloe. I've only just come out of a relationship, and I'm really not ready for another. I just want to enjoy being single."

"Well, guys like Damien are never single for long, so you better know what you're doing."

I have a feeling Chloe is right Damien is definitely someone special. But how do I know our relationship won't turn bad like it did with John.

We both freshen up in the bathroom and then get into bed, falling asleep as soon as our heads hit the pillows.

It is now Sunday morning, and I am so excited for my day with Chloe. First, we are going on an open-top bus tour. I cannot wait to see the sights properly. I have been in London a while now, but I haven't done anything touristy yet. Chloe has never been to London before, so we are both making the most of the tour. I am then going to take Chloe to an amazing restaurant by the Thames. It has the best reviews on Trip Advisor and is all over Instagram, apparently, which will impress Chloe. It isn't cheap, but I want to treat Chloe for everything she has done for me. Unfortunately, the waiting list for reservations is six months long. But the guys at work said if you get lucky and someone hasn't turned up, they will allow walk-ins, so fingers crossed. If not, there are plenty of other places we can go to.

We both walk out of the hotel giddy and excited for our day ahead.

"Wow, look at that limo, Bella. I wonder who that's waiting for? Some big-shot millionaire, no doubt. God, I'd love to be a millionaire for the day just to ride around London in one of those!"

A huge smile spreads across my face...

"Miss White, Miss Smith, your carriage awaits," George says as he tips his cap and opens the door to the sparkly black stretch Rolls Royce.

I look at Chloe, whose jaw is almost hitting the floor. I am so thankful I took Damien up on his offer.

"Thank you George." I beam.

We climb into the immaculate cream leather interior to find a bottle of champagne on ice, two champagne flutes, and a card that reads:

Ladies, I hope you enjoy your day. Please enjoy the champagne. George will be available all day if you may need him. D x

"Oh my God!" squeals Chloe as she grabs the champagne. It has a gold label and a name I have never heard of, but I imagine it is very expensive.

"Where to, ladies?" George asks as he re-enters the Rolls.

I give George the location of where we catch the bus tour, and we pull out into the London traffic. I explain the plan for the day, and Chloe gets so excited about what we are going to see. I tell her about the restaurant and how we need to keep our fingers crossed.

"Bella, this is already the best day ever. I don't mind if we eat at McDonald's!" she exclaims.

We have some time before the bus tour starts, so George takes us on a scenic route around

London. Not that we see much, as we are too busy drinking the champagne and chatting excitedly. We arrive at the bus stop, and I feel a little tipsy as the fresh air hits me. We thank George, and just as he pulls away, the open-top red double-decker bus arrives.

"Eeek! It's here!" Chloe says as she does a little dance on the pavement.

I could blame her over excitement on the champagne, but it has nothing to do with it, this is just typical Chloe. Another one of the reasons I love her. She is so confident, and she doesn't care what anyone thinks of her. She will talk to anyone and attracts people with her friendliness. I, on the other hand, feel constantly aware of people around me and what they may be thinking when they look at me. I'm shy and always worry about saying the wrong thing. I have to think about what I'm going to say before I say it, so sometimes, I just don't say anything. People mistake that for ignorance or rudeness.

Chloe has helped me so much with this anxiety over the years. She was the one who encouraged me to pursue my dream of being a hairdresser. It was something I'd dreamed of as a child, but I almost didn't do it. I was so scared of the actual interaction with people I didn't know. Chloe helped me explore lots of tips and techniques to overcome the anxiety. I still struggle with it, but not as much. I know how to power through it now.

Other people arrive at the bus stop and smile at Chloe, and she starts a conversation with an elderly gentleman who is on his own. You can see his spirit lift as she talks to him. I'm in awe of my best friend. We board the bus, and Chloe asks the gentleman if he would like to sit with us. He explains that he and his wife had this trip to London booked for six months, as it had been an anniversary present. He bought it for her, as she had never been to London. Unfortunately, she passed away before she was able to see the sights. So, he decided to come on his own. He told us that he almost didn't come today, but meeting Chloe had cheered him up already, and he knew he had made the right decision. This is just the type of person my best friend is.

We have a great day, hopping on and off the bus, taking selfies. We see Big Ben, the Houses of Parliament, and the Changing of the Guard at Buckingham Palace. This was quite an emotional experience, something I will never forget and definitely a must-see. Our tour ends with a Thames River cruise. We have such a great day. We make friends with the others on the tour (all thanks to Chloe) and laugh non-stop throughout. We say our goodbyes and head in the direction of the restaurant where I am hoping we can get a table. Chloe really wouldn't mind just getting some chips and sitting on a bench, but I really hope I can treat her. Plus, my legs are so tired now, I could do with a sit-down for a while.

We enter the restaurant, and the beauty of it dazzles as we walk in. It's like a tropical garden. The walls and ceiling are decorated with impressive greenery, crisp turquoise leaves, and colourful exotic flowers. There's a waterfall by the bar which sends sparkles of light all around the restaurant. We are greeted by the very glamorous, albeit snooty-looking, hostess. I explain that we don't have a reservation but am wondering if they have had any cancellations or if they could just squeeze the two of us in somewhere.

"I'm sorry, madam, but we do not 'squeeze' anyone in at Le Jardin, and we do not have any cancellations. I can book you in at our next available time, which will be in about six months?" she says, much to my disappointment.

My heart sinks, even though I'd thought it would probably be the case, but the hostess is so rude with her fake French accent that it really gets me down. The high I'd been on throughout the day has completely disappeared.

"Never mind. I fancy fish and chips anyway. Come on—let's find a Wetherspoons and get tipsy!" Chloe says as she puts her arm around me and gives me a squeeze, making me feel better as we head to the door.

"Excuse me, ladies. Excuse me?" says a gentleman who is making his way through the restaurant.

"I think he's talking to us, Bella?" Chloe stops, turning to see what he wants.

"I'm ever so sorry, ladies, there's has been a terrible mistake on our behalf," he says as he glares at the hostess. "Please accept my apologies. There is a table ready on the terrace for you. If you would like to follow me." He motions for us to follow him.

The gentleman is wearing a very smart suit and a badge that reads Restaurant Manager. I look at Chloe and then the hostess, and they both look as surprised as I am.

"You heard the man—after you, Bella," says Chloe as she ushers me to follow.

We walk out on to the terrace. The view overlooking over the Thames is spectacular. The manager shows us to our table, which must easily be the best vantage point in the restaurant. There must be some mistake—he must think we are someone else. I'm opening my mouth to explain the mistake when he addresses me directly.

"Miss White, I am terribly sorry about the confusion. Please accept a bottle of champagne on the house."

A waiter then rushes around him and sets it on the table in an ice bucket.

"Thank you, that's very kind," says Chloe with a big smile on her face.

I'm stunned into silence, and I'm not really sure what's going on. The waiter opens the champagne and pours us each a glass. They both then leave us with a menu. We look at each other and let out excited giggles.

"I don't understand, Chloe—I thought there

had been some mistake. I thought that he'd given us someone's table, thinking we were someone else, but he addressed me as Miss White. Did you hear him?"

Chloe rolls her eyes at me. "Yep! I understand perfectly. It's that sex god of yours. He did this. Definitely."

We each let out another laugh.

"Cheers!" we chorus and take big sips of our champagne.

We enjoy the most beautiful-looking food I have ever seen. The presentation and flavour are incredible. Most of it looks so pretty, I almost can't eat it. The view, the service—everything is just as I thought it would be and more. I'm so happy right now. Being here with Chloe, I have never felt so relaxed and content. We talk non-stop through our meal, but then Chloe drops a bombshell.

"Bella, we really need to talk about John," she says.

His name makes my stomach knot and fills me with anxiety. A feeling I have suffered every day for years. But then I realise that I haven't felt like this since I arrived in London—well, hardly.

"He's completely lost the plot. Your house is a mess—it's never going to sell in the state that it's in. John keeps disappearing for days—weeks, even. He's been fired from his job. His parents keep mithering me, asking me if I know where he is and asking me to get in contact with you. I really didn't want to burden you with this, Bella. But I don't know what else to do." Chloe takes hold of my hand and gives me a sympathetic smile. "I love how happy you are here, and it's such a long time since I have seen you this relaxed. You're back to just being you, the Bella we all know and love. Moving here was the best thing you have ever done. I miss you like crazy, but I would much rather you be here. Plus, I may be persuaded to move here too. It's actually not bad, this city life! Have you spoken to John since you moved?"

I'm shocked to hear about John. I still do care about him, and being fired from his job is just not like John at all. He loved his work, always worked hard, and took it very seriously. And the house—he was always a perfectionist. I'm surprised he's let it get to a state where Chloe would call it a mess.

"He messaged me a few times when I first moved here. He demanded I came home, and when I said I wasn't going to, he sent me some nasty messages, so I blocked him again. I'll ring the estate agent tomorrow and see what's going on."

"You should have told me about the messages, Bella. You know I'm always here for you. God, I wish I had got you away from him sooner. That time when he locked you in the bathroom all night and made you sleep on the floor—I should have packed your things then and not let you go back. I knew then he wasn't right in the head!" Chloe says with a sigh.

A sudden flashback of that evening comes over me. I went out with the girls into town. I got a dress a few days before that I felt really lovely in. I went shopping with my mum, and she kindly treated me to it. It was black, fitted, fell just above the knee, and had little cap shoulders and a sweetheart neckline. I felt confident and sexy in it, and my mum approved, so it wasn't too revealing.

John didn't like it, though. He said I looked like a slut and insisted I didn't wear it. I didn't have time to buy anything else, and I really didn't want to wear an old outfit. As John was still at work when I left to go out, I wore the dress. Two hours into the night, John turned up at the bar we were in and dragged me home. I told the girls it was fine and that I had a headache anyway, but Chloe knew that wasn't true.

When we got home, he ripped the dress from my body. He then threw me into the bathroom, where I hit my head on the sink and passed out. I woke up freezing later that night, lying on the bathroom floor in pitch-black darkness. I tried to open the door and discovered he had locked me in. I fumbled around and found a couple of towels and curled up on the floor. I sobbed all night, unable to sleep.

In the morning, John apologised profoundly, and me being me, I accepted and continued on. Chloe thought that was the first time anything like it had happened. It was definitely the worst up to that point, but it definitely wasn't the first. She also didn't know about him ripping the dress from me or the fact that I hit my head and had lain unconscious for God knows how long.

"It's not your fault," I tell her. "I always played everything down when it came to John—you weren't to know. I'll find out what's going on tomorrow, Chloe. Can we just forget about him for tonight and enjoy our time together? You're going home in the morning. It's gone by too fast. I've loved having you here."

"Me too. I'll be back soon—I've got unfinished business with that Josh guy anyway." Chloe shrugs and gives me a wink.

I ask for the bill and explain to Chloe that it's my treat. She protests at first until I promise she can get the next one.

"Ladies, how did you enjoy your meal this evening?" The manager who seated us has returned.

"It was all perfect, thank you," I say immediately.

"I'm extremely pleased to hear that, and please accept my apologies again for our little mix-up. Mr. King has already settled your bill, ladies, and the champagne was on the house. Please stay as long as you like and enjoy the rest of your evening."

I look at Chloe, who has the biggest smile on her face.

"I told you, Bella. He's a keeper. Now come on —let's go and get me even more drunk!"

We walk out of the restaurant, and George is there waiting for us. I know Damien means well, but it's all starting to feel a bit too much. Chloe looks so excited; therefore, I smile and climb in after her. George drops us off at a bar near the hotel. It's Sunday night, and it's really busy—well, every night is busy in London. We manage to find a couple of seats at the bar. I order us some cocktails, and Chloe brings me up to speed on all the gossip back home.

But I just can't relax. I have this weird anxious feeling that I just can't shake. Maybe it's because of the conversation we had earlier about John. Every so often I get a feeling I'm being watched. I turn to where I sense the gaze is coming from, but I don't see anyone. Well, I see lots of people, as it's extremely busy, but no one who looks familiar or seems to be looking back at me.

"I'm just nipping to the loo. You stay here and watch our seats then you can go," Chloe says.

I get my phone out and send a quick text to Damien thanking him for his generosity tonight, but I also tell him it's too much. Something is really bothering me tonight, and I can't put my finger on what it is. It's possibly a mixture of things. Chloe returns, so I down the rest of my drink and go to the toilet myself.

All the alcohol in the cocktail must have settled at the bottom of the glass. It almost made me gag, it was so bitter. I stand in the queue for the toilet and start to feel really dizzy. Finally, it's my turn. I spend a penny and reach for the cubicle door. Strangely, my arms are so heavy I can hardly lift them to open the lock. I keep trying and almost reach it, but my arm drops and so does the rest of my body. I feel myself hit the cold floor, and everything goes black.

Chapter 10

Damien.

I've been working late tonight. We've a lot going on within King Security. We are about to expand, and there is still a lot to do. I call it a night and am retiring to my bedroom when my phone rings. It's Josh.

"Hi, mate. There's been an issue tonight with one of the teams at Bar Seven. A girl passed out in the bathroom, and the guys had to break the door down to get her out. They got her an ambulance because her mate was kicking up such a fuss, saying her drink must have been tampered with. The guys rang me to check the bar footage, as this girl's mate was adamant that someone had spiked her drink, and we needed to call the police to report it. I got the footage sent over, and I'm looking at it now. The girl's drink is definitely spiked. She's at the bar on her own, messaging on her phone, and a guy reaches round her and puts something in her drink. When her mate returns, she downs the drink and then goes to the toilet. It must have been a lot or some strong shit because within minutes, she was out," he explains.

"So, ring the police and hand them the footage. Why are you ringing me with this, Josh?" I respond, disgruntled.

"Because the girls in video are Bella and Chloe," Josh replies.

I immediately panic. "I need to get to hospital now!"

"I'm outside. I'll drive you," Josh says calmly.

Josh didn't say which of the girls had been drugged, but I know it's Bella. I feel it in my stomach. I don't know Bella's condition, but it can't be good. We arrive at A&E, and I see Chloe talking to a nurse.

"She's awake now. You can go in and see her."

Chloe looks relieved as the nurse speaks. Josh pulls Chloe into a hug, and she starts to cry on his shoulder.

"Is she okay, Chloe? What the hell happened?!" I demand.

She pulls away from Josh and looks at me. "I thought I lost her, Damien. When we arrived at the hospital, she started fitting, and all these alarms went off, and they took her away and said I was to stay here."

"How is she now?" I ask.

"The nurse said we can go and see her and that she's awake. She's through here."

I follow Chloe, but Josh stays in the waiting area—I'm assuming to make some calls and find out who the hell did this. My blood is boiling. I feel like finding the person responsible and ripping his head off. But now I need to be calm and make sure Bella is well. When we enter the room, I'm relieved to see Bella awake.

"Hey there. You gave us all a scare." Chloe strokes her head as she speaks to her.

"I'm sorry, I don't know what happened. I went to the toilet, and then it all went black. I didn't think I had drunk that much."

She looks so tiny and fragile in that big hospital bed. She has tubes up her nose and in her arms. The anger and hurt inside me at seeing her like this is something I haven't felt for anyone other than my parents.

"Bella, you had your drink spiked. I have Josh and our guys working on it now. We will find the arsehole who did this to you. I am sure it was just a random attack, so you mustn't worry. Just concentrate on getting better," I say as I kiss her on the top of her head. "I am going to go and help Josh. I've one of the guys on route to the hospital now. He will stay here until you leave. As I said, I am sure it was just random, but just for everyone's peace of mind, he will come. No doubt the police will be here soon to talk to you about the incident. My guy will be there to get rid of them if it gets too much. You have my number. If you need anything at all, just ring. I also have Penny on her way with some necessities. When she gets here, you can ask her to get anything from your apartment too."

Bella looks at me, clearly overwhelmed. She smiles a tired little smile and thanks me. I nod and leave the room. I need to see that footage for myself and get my hands on this guy's throat. I find Josh in the waiting area with one of the team. He's briefed on what we need him to do. Josh and I leave and head to Bar Seven. I also want to know how this has even happened under my watch.

I go through the video footage, and clear as day, a guy in a cap drops something into Bella's drink.

"Boss, we've got him," says a King Security employee.

I follow him out of the room into the bar's office to see the guy from the video facing me. He's looking very worse for wear—a burst lip, a bloody nose, and an eye that he will struggle to open for a few days. He looks up as I enter.

"Seriously, mate, I've told your guys all I know. This guy came up to me and said he'd give me a hundred quid to put something in some bird's drink. I'm a shit, I know, but I needed the money. You've got to listen to me, mate—I never meant to hurt anyone!"

"First of all, I'm not fucking your mate." I give the guy a fist to the face. He will now have matching eyes in the morning. The guy continues to apologise, but he doesn't mean it, he is just trying to save himself.

"Do we have a description of this other guy?" I ask my men.

"Yes, boss."

"Good!"

WHACK! I crack the imbecile around the head again, and he's out for the night.

"Get him out of here and find me the guy who paid him!" I demand.

"Right on it, boss."

Seething, I leave the office and return to Josh.

"Josh, I'm not sure why or who, but someone wanted to hurt Bella on purpose tonight. I need this to be the team's main priority until we find out what's going on. I want eyes on Bella twenty-four seven."

Josh looks at me like I am overreacting, which maybe I am, but he knows not to question me.

Back at my apartment, I feel a wave of homesickness—or is it loneliness? I am not sure. I pour myself a scotch and rack my brains, trying to think of who would want to hurt Bella, and I keep coming to the same conclusion. Someone is trying to get to me through her.

Being in the business I am, I quite often make enemies. But the person whom I most suspect is Pete. He reared his ugly head at my dad's funeral, and now this. But how would he know about her? My mind is going around in circles, and I'm so frustrated. Feeling the need to check on Bella, I ring Dave, who was the one assigned to watch her in hospital. He informs me she's sleeping, and he is outside her room. The doctors said she will be able to come home tomorrow. But she needs to be looked after. Chloe must get back to work, and Bella hasn't told her parents what happened, as she doesn't want them to worry. I decide Bella will come and stay with me. That way I can keep an eye on her.

When I arrive at the hospital the next day, Bella has just finished her lunch and is looking much more like her usual self. She gives me one of her smiles that do something to my heart. She's not fond of the idea of staying with me—of course she likes her independence. But after some persuasion from me as well as the doctor advising her she can't go home alone, she agrees. I decide to take her to my family home, Kingston Manor.

Kingston is on its own grounds, and the security is very tight. We pull up to the gate entrance, and I put my window down.

"Good afternoon, Mr. King. Miss." The member of the security team nods and dips his cap to Bella. "It's good to see you, sir. My deepest condolences. Your father is greatly missed."

"Indeed, he is. Thank you," I reply.

The gates open, and I drive down the tree-lined stone driveway. It's a minute or two before the trees start to clear and you get a view of the house.

Bella gasps and her eyes widen. "Damien, is this your house?" she asks, full of amazement.

"Yes. It belonged to my parents and now to me. It's a breath taker, isn't it. Even after spending most of my childhood here, I'm still in awe when I return. I never appreciated it as a child, but I have so many happy memories of growing up here with my family," I say with fondness.

Bella's eyes meet mine, and I feel a well of emotion. What is wrong with me? I look away and shake it off.

George is waiting to greet us. He opens Bella's door and stretches his hand out to help her from the car.

"Good afternoon, Miss White," he says in his most gentlemanly voice.

"Please, George—call me Bella."

George nods, accepting her request. I walk round the car and pass the keys to him. I pick Bella up with a clean swoop. I carry her up the steps and through the double wooden doors.

"Damien, I can walk, you know—put me down!" Bella giggles and smacks my shoulder playfully.

"No, you are going straight to your room. You have just come out of hospital, you've had a busy day of being poked and prodded, and it was only last night you almost.... Well, you gave us all a fright. I am putting you to bed, and whatever you need, I will wait on you hand and foot. Your wish is my command," I say as I carry my Bella through the house and up the stairs to my bedroom. Watching Bella's face as she takes in the house has me smiling. I can't wait to show her around properly once she's up to it.

As I lay her on the bed, she lets out a yawn.

"You need to sleep, beautiful."

I take off her shoes, then pull back the covers for her to snuggle in. When I stand up to leave her, she grabs my hand.

"Damien, don't go, please. Will you lie with me?" she innocently asks.

How can I say no? I kick off my shoes and lie down beside her. She cuddles up to me and rests her cheek on my chest. I kiss the top of her head and breathe her in. That smell, that sweet smell that makes me feel like I'm home. We fall asleep in each other's arms.

When I wake, the room is pitch-black. My watch tells me it's 8:00 p.m. I hadn't realised how tired I was. Ordinarily I have trouble sleeping, but next to Bella, sleep comes so easy.

Bella starts to stir.

"Hey there, beautiful. How are you feeling?" Kissing her forehead, I give her a little squeeze.

"Good, I think. I'm a little hungry," she says with a stretch.

I'm glad she is. Bella's had her stomach pumped and been on all sorts of drips to flush out her system. Being hungry is a good sign.

"Me too. What do you fancy?" I ask.

"I'm not sure. What have you got?" she replies.

I chuckle in response. There's nothing Bella could ask for that Penny wouldn't have in the kitchen, and if we don't have it, George will ensure we get it.

"Knowing Penny, she has probably prepared us something. I will call down and see." Within minutes of speaking to Penny, we have a trolley in our room, full of homemade soups, sandwiches, and cakes, along with a selection of drinks.

"This is incredible, Penny. Thank you, but you really shouldn't have gone to all this trouble for me," Bella says.

"It's no trouble at all—we need to build your strength up. Now is there anything else I can get for the two of you?" Penny asks.

"I think we will be just fine for the evening now, Penny. Thank you." I give Peny an appreciative smile.

Penny leaves us, and I serve us both some food. I enjoy watching Bella eat. She really enjoys her food. The little faces she makes and her noises of appreciation amuse me to no end. Once we finish, I run Bella a bath. While she is relaxing, I go to my home office and ring Josh to see if he has any updates for me. To my disappointment, he does not.

Bella

This bathroom is out of this world! I'm lying in a bath that could easily fit four people. It's all white marble with glittery grey veins running through it. The taps are mini water falls that come out of the wall. There's a television screen and some kind of iPad with buttons on the built-in beside the tub. I have no idea what that's for, therefore I won't be touching it. The smell of my bubbles is divine; it's the signature range from the King Hotel, obviously. This is the perfect place to relax, but for some reason, I can't. I feel so.... I'm not sure how I feel. On edge? Overwhelmed?

I haven't told my parents that my drink was spiked or that I've been in hospital. Which makes me feel guilty. But they would just worry and insist on me going home. Maybe I should have told them? Maybe I should have gone home? Damien has been amazing. He didn't need to look after me like this, as we haven't known each other for long.

That being said, we do seem to have a connection. I'm just a little apprehensive, as he is so dominating with me, albeit in a good way. It's taken me years to get out of a relationship where I had been controlled, and although I know Damien is nothing like John, his dominance started to ring alarm bells. It's making me panic slightly. It's just that meeting Damien and getting so close happened so quickly. I don't even know what this is between us. Are we in a relationship?

The bath isn't doing much good for my anxiety, so I get out, dry off, and put on my pjs. I lie on the bed and ring Chloe and Katie in turn to let them know how I am. Katie's doing some extra hours at the salon to take care of some of my clients; she has rearranged the rest. I'll have a few busy weeks when I go back, but I don't mind. The doctor at the hospital signed me off sick for a week. I'm sure I won't need that long, but I'll do as I'm told. As soon as I put down the phone, I suddenly feel really sick. I dash to the toilet and make it just in time.

"Bella? Bella? Are you okay?" Damien's standing at the door.

Great, I must look a complete mess, hugging the toilet with sick dripping off my chin. Oh no—here it comes again. I throw up again, but this time Damien is beside me, holding my hair and rubbing my back. I'm there for a few minutes, saying hello again to everything I just ate—nice. Once I'm sure there's nothing left in my stomach, Damien passes me a cloth for my face. He helps me up and takes me over to the sink. I brush my teeth and rinse my mouth. Throughout, Damien's hands are on my back, taking my weight. My legs feel like jelly, and my head is pounding. Once I'm finished, Damien picks me up and puts me in bed.

"The doctor said this might happen. Your stomach is weak from being pumped and the drugs you ingested. He said you may get a headache too. Do you have one?"

"Yep," I say as I hold my head. I need to sleep. Damien passes me some water. I take a sip and snuggle into him. I'm soon fast asleep.

When I wake up in the morning, I'm alone. I pick up my phone and check the time. 7:30 a.m. I can't hear Damien in the bathroom, so he must have gone downstairs—or upstairs. I'm not sure how many floors this house has. I would get up and find him, but I'm afraid I'll get lost. I sit up and take in the room around me. I feel so small in this queen-size bed. The mattress is so soft, it moulds around me. I'm surrounded by feather pillows and crisp white sheets. The headboard is covered with gold-and-bronze velvet. It's padded in geometric shapes and goes right up to the high ceiling. At each side of the headboard, there are alcoves with shelves containing sculptures that are lit from top to bottom with spotlights.

Opposite the bed there are three windows —a huge floor-to-ceiling one in the middle and two smaller ones on either side. The window on the left has a window seat with silky white-and-bronze-striped cushions. The one on the right has a dressing table in front of it. I won't be doing my makeup in here, though, that's for sure—not with this carpet. The carpet—well, it's more like a full floor rug—is pure white, and the pile is so thick that when I put my feet on it, my toes disappear.

I get out of bed and walk around the room, enjoying how it feels under my feet. Never mind hoover lines—this carpet leaves footprints. I sit on the window seat and look out to the back of the house. Well, I'm assuming it's the back—it could be the side. The house and grounds are so big. There's a large patio area with steps going down to an expansive lawn with a big fountain in the middle in which birds are drinking and bathing. The garden is beautifully kept with colourful roses and other pretty flowers that I don't know the names of. It stretches as far as my eyes can see, a wall of green with spots of colour. To the left I spot what looks like a stable and a barn.

"Good morning, you're awake. How did you sleep?" Damien asks, looking pleased to see me.

Unable to quite get my words out, mesmerised by the sight in front of me, I just smile and nod. Damien is stood filling the doorway. He must have been doing some kind of workout, as his skin is flushed and sparkles with sweat, and he looks completely edible. He is wearing a white T-shirt and black short shorts. You know, the little ones rugby players wear that show every curve and every bulge. Oh my, that bulge. These shorts leave nothing to the imagination. I lick my lips, then realise I'm staring. My eyes move up to his, and he has a little smirk on his face as if he knows what I'm thinking.

"I'm going to shower, and then we will go down for breakfast," he says whilst kissing the top of my head. He smells all manly and delicious.

We have breakfast in the dining room. There's fresh fruit and pastries laid out on the table. Damien has a full English, but I stick to a small bowl of cereal—I don't want an upset tummy again. The dining room is very grand. I'm sure many wonderful dinner parties have taken place here.

After we eat, Damien takes me on a tour of

the house. There's a gym and a swimming pool, a cinema room and games room. I can't quite believe I am here or that I know someone who actually owns a place like this.

We stroll out into the garden.

"You have a very beautiful home," I admit.

"Thank you. My father had it built for me and my mother. He designed it himself. I have lots of happy memories of growing up here. When my parents passed, they left it to me. I haven't been back here since my mother passed away, and my father hadn't either. He came to live in New York with me when my mother died. It's a very big, lonely house when you're on your own," he explains, clearly struck with deep sentiment.

"I'm sorry, Damien. Has it been hard for you coming back here with me? You know I would have been perfectly fine at my apartment—"

"No!" Damien interjects suddenly.

I jump a little, taken back by the loudness of his voice.

"Sorry, I don't mean to be abrupt. I want to take care of you, Bella. I have needed to come here for a long time. But I've been worried how I would feel. I worried that the house would feel so empty and not welcoming, unlike when my mother was here. This is why I wanted you here—you make it feel…. Well, you make me feel…." Damien stumbles over his words. "It doesn't matter. This was the best place for you to recover, and I won't hear another word about it," he commands.

Just when I think he's letting me in, he shuts me back out. I smile to myself, though, as I know what he meant; he makes me feel like that too.

We decide to go for a swim. I've got a bikini on and a robe over the top. Penny brought me everything I could possibly need clothes-wise and toiletries as well. Damien is already in the pool. I suddenly feel very nervous—shy, even? Damien has seen me naked before, but this feels really scary, like my whole body is on display.

My bikini is white, and I still have a bit of a tan. Although I've not been to the gym in a while, I'm still in pretty good shape. I never have really worried about how my body looked in a bikini before, but I realise that I'm nervous about how Damien will see my body. He's so handsome, muscular, and toned. He must have been with some very beautiful women. I hope he isn't put off by my silvery stretch marks and curvy bottom.

"Come on in—the water's not cold," Damien shouts as he swims over to me.

I take a deep breath, remove my robe, and slide in. As soon as I enter the water, Damien is beside me. He puts his hands on my waist and stares into my eyes. Reassuringly, I see nothing but desire. His lips meet mine with passion and force. His tongue enters my mouth, claiming it as his own. His hands move down to my bum, and he lifts me. I wrap my legs around him. Tightening my thighs, I feel his erection pulsing between us.

His mouth moves to my neck, and his trail

of kisses and nibbles sends shivers down my body. "I'm sorry, Bella, I cannot resist any longer—I need to taste you. I need to be inside you."

His desperation for me pulls at my heart. I am putty in his hands.

"Take me, Damien," I utter breathlessly.

I don't need to ask him twice. He pulls my bikini pants to the side, and with one deep thrust, he is inside me. I cry out at the sudden stretch and fullness, but it feels so right, like I had been empty without him.

He holds himself still and gives me a minute to adjust while making love to my mouth with his. The pleasure and emotions I feel right now, I never knew were even possible. He begins to thrust, slowly at first. I can tell he's trying his hardest to hold back, but he's as hungry as I am for this. The sound of splashing water and cries of pleasure echo around the room. I take in every feeling, every sensation, every sound. I'm not sure how long this "relationship" will last with Damien, but I am storing everything in my memory so that I will never forget it.

Once we come down from our euphoria, I reassure Damien for the hundredth time he was not to too rough and I am more than fine.

"It was perfect, Damien. You are perfect."

We kiss for a little longer before climbing out of the water to dry off. We lie covered in towels on some comfy loungers by the pool and cuddle up.

"I need to go back home this weekend. There are some things I need to sort out regarding my house. Plus I'd really like to see my family," I explain.

"Would you like me to come with you?" Damien asks protectively.

"No, thank you. Not this time, anyway. It's complicated. I own the house with my ex-boyfriend John." Gosh, the thought of him now suddenly gives me a range of emotions—anger, sadness, anxiety, even sympathy? I'm realising more and more how toxic our relationship was. I feel so foolish. "Our breakup wasn't the easiest, and we don't have any contact with each other now. Our house is on the market, but Chloe said he's not been looking after it and he keeps disappearing for weeks, so there've been no viewings. I need to go and see it for myself as well as speak to the estate agent and to him."

The thought of seeing him makes my stomach turn. Damien just listens. He's nodding and looking intently at my face as if trying to read me. I have never spoken to him about John before—I've tried to block him out of my mind, really.

Damien gives me a big squeeze and kisses the top of my head. "I'm here if you need me. Anything at all, just ask," he says. I know he means every word. I feel so grateful to have a man who wants to take care of me. However, this I need to do on my own.

The days at Kingston fly by. It's a wonderful time of relaxing, eating, swimming, walking, cuddling, talking, and making love. Love is indeed what I'm feeling now, and it's really scaring me. I feel loved and I'm most definitely falling in love. Damien has made me feel so welcome in his home and has treated me like a princess. But I just feel like it is all too good to be true. I feel like this fairy tale will end, that I don't belong in his life. I need to speak to Damien about where this is going because I need to protect my heart. I've been through so much emotionally, and I don't know if my heart or brain could take much more pain.

Damien has helped me realise a lot of things about my relationship with John and about myself. I will never let myself be controlled the way I was or be treated in such a way that I feel worthless. Whatever this is with Damien, it has made me stronger, and I won't ever put myself down again. I'm going to go back home his weekend, and then I will speak to Damien when I come back. I want to keep my little fairy-tale bubble intact for a little longer.

Chapter 11

Bella

The tube station is extremely busy today. I am once again filled with anxiety as I start my journey back to Lancashire. The train pulls up, and everyone pushes to get on. I'm knocked forwards and backwards and from side to side. I can't breathe. My chest is tight, and I can hear my heartbeat in my ears. I push back, trying get out of the crowd to find some air. I stand against the brick wall and catch my breath. Wow, I suddenly realise that I haven't felt like this in such a long time. I think the last time was the day I moved to London. I wasn't prepared. I have forgotten how to deal with it.

I stay there for about five minutes. A couple more trains pull in and out, and people rush and push to get on. I take some deep breaths and stand behind the yellow line, feet firmly on the ground, and when the train pulls up, I forcefully make my way on. Thankfully there's a seat near the doors, so sit hugging my bag and feeling relieved that I made it. It may seem so trivial to some, but I'm proud of myself for not letting my anxiety stop me from doing I want to do.

The rest of the journey is much easier. I'm in control. I check and double-check the times and platforms one hundred times, but that's how I stay in control. After a short taxi ride from the station I'm here, walking up the driveway of my parent's bungalow. My mum opens the door as I approach.

"Bella, sweetheart, how are you? I've missed you!" she says as she pulls me into a big hug.

"I've missed you, too, Mum," I say, breathing her in.

"Come on in. How was your trip? Are you hungry? What can I get you to drink?" she asks.

I smile. This is my mum—always trying to feed everyone. She's so loving and motherly. She is the most caring and selfless person I have ever met. Growing up, I thought all mums were like this; now I'm older, I realise how lucky I am.

"I'd love a cup of tea, please."

. My dad's in the lounge his usual chair.

"Come here and give your old man a hug." We give each other a squeeze before I take a seat on the sofa.

Mum returns with china cups of tea on saucers and a plate of biscuits

I tell them my news and how much I'm enjoying working and living in London. They look so proud and happy for me. They make "oooh" and "wow" sounds when I describe everything.

"We are so proud of you, sweetheart. It's so lovely to see you so happy."

And though I know that she means every word, my mum definitely wishes I live closer. I know she misses me terribly, but she would never tell me that. She saw how unhappy I was before I left and knows that this is the best place for me at the moment.

"What are your plans for today, Bella?" she asks.

"Well, I need to go to the house and see John. I'm not sure what's been going on. I rang the estate agent on the train up here. She said she has numerous people interested in it, but she can't ever get hold of John to arrange a viewing. She said one time she went to the house, as he wasn't answering the phone, and knocked on the door. Apparently, he answered and shouted at her to leave and used some very obscene words," I explain.

"I'll come with you. I've never liked that guy," says my dad, but that's a fib.

He did like him—everyone does. Well, did. Something has happened to John over the years; he's changed. Then again, we were just eighteen when we met, so he was never going to be the same person as an adult, I suppose.

"I'll be fine, Dad. I need to speak to him on my own. Thank you, though," I say.

When I walk up to my house, I'm upset to see it looks so dark and sad. The blinds are all shut, and the lawn is overgrown and covered in weeds.

The window boxes have large dandelions growing out of them. I've never seen it this way before. We both used to be so house proud—we spent most weekends pottering outside. Don't get me wrong, I'm no gardener, and I have no idea about plant names, etc., but I know what's a weed, and I like pretty, colourful flowers.

John's car is on the drive. Chloe says she has seen him around the last few days, so I'm expecting him to be here. As I start walking down the path, the front door opens.

"Bella! I knew you'd come home. I knew you would see sense and come back to me," John says grinning.

"Hi, John. Can I come in?" I ask.

He moves aside, and I walk into the front room.

"I've not come back to stay," I clarify. "I've come to talk to you and help sort the house out so we can get it sold. You know that's what I want. It's what we both need—a fresh start."

"It's not what I want. You belong to me. I mean, you belong here with me. I love you, Bella—we belong together. Just please stay and let us work this mess out," he says, clearly full of pain.

This is going to be harder than I thought.

"I'm sorry, but I'm happy where I am in London. I've moved on, and you need to too," I say, looking around and noticing the place is a mess. There are takeaway boxes everywhere, plates and cups covered in mouldy food, photo frames smashed on the floor. The smell is stale, and it looks like it's not been cleaned since I was last here. "John, what has happened? This isn't like you. You're normally so tidy."

He slumps down on the sofa in response, drops his head into his hands, and begins to cry. He really sobs. "I'm sorry, Bella—I just can't live without you. You've been by my side my whole adult life, and I don't know how to function without you. I've lost my job. I can't pay the bills. I am nothing without you. I need you."

I sit on the sofa beside him and wrap an arm around him. He leans into me and cries into my shoulder. At first, I can't help but feel responsible for him being this way. I just left him; he thought we would be together forever, but then he puts his hand on my leg and I freeze in panic. Memories of what those hands have done to me come flooding back. I'm stronger now though, I tell myself. "We will get you some help. Everything will be okay." I sit with him for a minute, rubbing his back, knowing as long as I keep him calm everything will be fine. I will sort the house out and then I never have to be this close to him again. "First of all, let's get this house cleaned up," I say as he calms down. He nods and stands up.

Over the next few hours, we work together, gathering up all the rubbish, washing the pots, and giving everything a good clean. John starts to seem more like himself, and I hope that I might be getting somewhere with him. He takes out the rubbish, and when he comes back in, he locks the back door and puts the key in his pocket.

I'm not sure why he needed to do that. I think it's time I should be going.

"Well, that looks much better, doesn't it?" I say as I look around the house. "Right, I'm going to get off now, John. I'm going to speak to your family, and together we will make sure you're all right. Everything will be okay." I take off the rubber gloves I've been wearing and put them under the sink.

"I know everything will be okay, because you're not going anywhere," he says suddenly.

I look at him, nervously, trying not to show the fear building inside of me He's got that evil glint in his eyes again. A sick feeling in my stomach I haven't felt for a long time sends me into panic mode.

"Yes, I am. I'm going back to my parents now, and then tomorrow I am going back to London. I will call in tomorrow and check on you," I say firmly as I walk to the front door. I pull the handle, but its locked. There's no key in the door. Frantically I look around for keys. But I don't see any. "Have you got the key for the door?" I ask, but he doesn't answer me. He just stands there looking at me with this strange expression on his face. "Open the door, John—you can't keep me here. My parents know I am here, and they will come looking for me."

John shakes his head and smiles such an evil

grin, he reminds me of the Grinch. "When they arrive, you will tell them you have made a terrible mistake and that you still love me. You will say you are staying here and that we are getting married. And you will make it believable."

He's insane.

"Why would I say that?" I inquire, trying to keep my calm.

"Because if you don't, I will make sure your parents pay."

Okay, this is bad. "Don't be ridiculous—they will never believe that!"

Trying to be discreet, I reach around to get my phone out of the back pocket of my jeans, but it's gone.

"You looking for this?" He holds up my phone. "You had a message from someone called Damien. Have you been cheating on me, Bella?"

He looks furious. He starts shouting in my face, calling me awful things. I feel myself burning up. I feel faint and sick. He throws my phone across the room. It smashes into pieces—there's no way it's going to save me now. I've been in this situation before. If I do as he asks, he will calm down.

"Damien is just a friend, that's all," I assure him in a soft voice.

"Aarrgghh! You've slept with him, haven't you! Haven't you?" he screams, pulling my hair so hard and tilting my face up to his. I cry out at the pain. "This is mine!" He grabs me between my legs.

I scream and shout for help. Fighting for

my life, I hit and kick him as much as I can, but he slams my head into the door. The pain sends a ringing into my ears. I remember the back-door key is in his pocket. I try and grab it, but he's too strong for me. He pushes me to the floor.

BANG! BANG! BANG! Someone is at the front door.

John grabs me and covers my mouth with his hand. "Be quiet, or this will end so much worse," he whispers in my ear.

BANG! BANG! BANG!

"OPEN THIS DOOR NOW, OR I WILL KNOCK IT DOWN!" a male voice I don't recognise bellows.

"Stay here and don't move," John grunts.

Like hell I am; as soon as he opens that door, I'll scream and run.

John puts the chain on and opens the door slightly "What do you want—"

BANG! The man kicks the door. It breaks the chain and swings open. I jump up and make a run for it. I push past John and the man standing in the doorway. He's a big guy dressed all in black. John tries to grab me, but the man holds on to him. I don't stop to thank him—I just run.

Running as fast as my legs can carry me, I cut through the alleyways and down the estate to my parents' house, thank goodness they live so close. When I get to the house, I'm in such a state I have no choice but to tell them what's happened. My dad is furious and goes round there. I beg him not to go, but he's always been stubborn. Mum and

I chase after him, but he took the car, so we have no option but to run. When we get there, the front door is open. Dad is in the living room, standing over John. There's blood all over his face, and he's not moving.

"What have you done?!" my mother shrieks.

"It wasn't me," Dad says "Somebody beat me to it. I've phoned the police, and an ambulance is on its way."

Chapter 12

Bella

On the train ride back to London, I decide I'm not going to tell Damien what happened with John. Thankfully and surprisingly, I don't have any marks where he hurt me. My mum made me go to A&E to be checked over, and they gave me a clean bill of health. I gave a statement to the police, and I now have a restraining order against John. Nobody knows who they guy that came to the house was. The police assume it is someone John owes money to, seeing as he is so much debt. I'm just glad he came when he did.

I collected my phone and thankfully it was repairable, but after going back there I have decided I don't want anything to do with that house anymore. My dad is speaking to a solicitor to get my name off the mortgage. I have also spoken to John's parents. Although they didn't really believe what I told them, they have agreed to get him some help. I can't wait to get back to London now and forget about this weekend. Damien has texted me, and he is picking me up from Euston. I'm pleased I don't have to get on the tube. I've had enough trauma for this week.

As I walk to the station's exit, I see Damien waiting. He's looking around for me. He hasn't spotted me yet, so I stand still for a moment and take him in. I can't believe that fine specimen of a man is waiting for me. He stands out in the crowd. Women can't take their eyes off him and men do a double-take. He towers above most people. His dark hair is swept back, his big dark eyes sparkle in the light, and that strong jaw has a five o'clock shadow. He's wearing a tight white T-shirt with a low neck. I could literally eat him all up. I never understood that expression before I met Damien. Now I fully understand—I could definitely eat him all up right now!

He spots me, and I smile; he smirks and raises one eyebrow. I think he just busted me ogling him—oh well. Damien gives me a one-armed hug and kisses the top of my head. I lean in and squeeze him back with my free arm.

"It's good to see you. Give me your bag," he says.

Once we are in the car and have set off driving, Damien starts to ask questions, which makes me anxious. I don't like lying, and I'm not very good at it.

"How was your weekend?" he asks.

"Yeah, good. It was great to see Mum and Dad," I reply, not looking at him.

"And how did it go with your ex regarding the house?"

"Fine, yeah—I've got my dad taking care of now, so hopefully I'll soon be rid of it and him," I say.

Damien remains silent. I look at him, and he looks back at me as if he's angry. I wonder whether he can see through my lies. Well, they weren't exactly lies—just not the whole truth.

"Is that it?" he asks.

"What do you mean?"

"Why are you lying to me, Bella?"

I study him, trying to work out what he knows. He looks furious.

"I haven't 'lied,' Damien," I insist.

"Well, you're not telling me the truth! You're not telling me about what that arsehole did to you!"

I'm not sure how he knows this? Maybe Chloe got in contact with him somehow. I'm not sure.

"I didn't want to worry you, Damien. I'm fine —he just went a little off the rails, but he's getting some help now."

"OFF THE RAILS!" he cries, banging the steering wheel.

"Damien, please stop! You're scaring me."

He pulls the car to the left down a back street and parks up.

"I'm sorry, I'm just so mad, Bella. God knows what could have happened to you if Gary had not intervened."

"I'm sorry, who?" I demand. It's all starting

to fall into place now. The guy who saved me by banging on the door. He wasn't there by accident. He had been sent by Damien. Thinking back, he was dressed just as one of the King Security team would be.

"You had someone following me?!" I say, feeling overwhelmed.

"Yes, for your own protection, and it's a flaming good job I did!" Damien snaps.

I'm furious. Obviously, I am now grateful for the fact that he sent him (although I won't be admitting that to him any time soon), but how could he have known what was going to happen with John? He didn't know I was in danger. So, he was actually having me followed.

"Damien, you can't do that! You can't just have me followed. I need my privacy. I just got out of a controlling relationship, goddamn it, and I will not stand for being controlled again!"

I'm breaking now—tears are streaming down my face. The reality of the weekend and my relationship with John is finally hitting me. I can't breathe, my chest is tight, and I need air. I need to get out of this car. I undo my belt and open the door. It's raining, but I don't care. I get out and run. There's a field at the side of the road. I climb over the fence and run through the long grass. I keep going until I can't breathe anymore, and my legs give way.

I'm down on my knees for what feels like only seconds before Damien's strong arms pick me up and rest me in his lap. He puts my head on his chest, then wraps his arms around me and just holds me. The rain pours down on us both, and I know his bum must be wet through, sitting on the ground. He rocks us slightly and squeezes me.

When I relax a little and my breathing returns to almost normal, Damien lifts my face to meet his.

"I'm sorry, Bella. When I heard you were hurt, my heart hurt too. I do not know what it is about you, but when I look at you, when I am around you, I feel.... I feel like I'm... home. I've never felt at home anywhere since my mother died. Home is not a place, Bella—home is where the heart is, and my heart is with you."

I have never seen Damien look so beautiful. There are raindrops dripping from his eyelashes and nose. His eyes are wide open. They're honest and safe, and I see my home in them. I know that every word he just said is true, and I know this because I feel it too. Home is not a place. It is the people who you are with that make a home.

"My heart is with you too. But I'm just so scared. I don't think I could take any more pain." I admit.

"I will never hurt her Bella." I really want to believe him.

Chapter 13

Bella

The weeks are passing quickly. I am really busy at work. My client base just keeps growing. I'm booked up weeks in advance now. In my evenings, I'm working on my hair for the show, which is only a week off now.

Damien's got a lot on with work too. They're expanding in London and working on a big case that seems to be top secret. Damien just changes the subject when I ask about it, which is fine. It goes with the line of work he is in, I suppose. We still manage to make time for each other, though. I don't think we've spent a night apart since the rainy field incident. We are still trying to keep things private between us; it's difficult with Damien being who he is. Obviously, Katie and Chloe know, but they're sworn to secrecy. Things are great at the moment. I'm feeling so happy. My relationship is good, and my career is everything I have ever dreamed it would be.

Until today, that is. Today things start to get a little strange.

"Bella, your client is here," calls Sarah from reception.

"Great, thank you. I'll be there in a minute," I reply as I set up my section for my first client of the day.

"Bella, your client is here," she says again.

"Yes, thank you—I'll be there in just a moment," I say more loudly, as she mustn't have heard me the first time.

"Bella, there's another client here for you?"

I walk into the reception area, and I have three clients waiting for me.

How did this happen? We have an all-singing, all-dancing, electronic booking system. There shouldn't ever be a mix-up, especially with three clients. But I do not let it phase me. I apologise to the clients, check my schedule, and squeeze them into my already jam-packed day. Unfortunately, today of all days, Rebecca our manager is in, and I feel like she is watching me like a hawk.

The next day goes from bad to worse. I'm doing one of my regular clients, a very particular lady in her fifties who obviously has a lot of money. She knows how she wants her hair, and it must be perfect. Definitely not one of my favourite clients, but she is a good tipper and books in with me every week for one thing or another. Today I've done her highlights, and the assistant has shampooed her. She's now waiting for me to apply her toner. I give the client record card to the assistant and ask her to mix the toner for me, as I am still finishing off my other client. I'm rushed off my feet and running behind again. As well as the extra clients, my appointment length times have been reduced unrealistically, and I just can't keep up.

When I get to Mrs. Particular, she's not impressed, as she's been waiting three and a half minutes with wet hair. I apologise and apply her toner, listening to her drone on about the new yacht her husband just bought. I've applied the sides and m halfway through applying the back when Mrs. Particular lets out an ear-splitting scream.

"My hair—it's turning PINK!"

I look into the mirror in front of her, and sure enough, her hair is turning a lovely shade of candy-floss pink.

"I'm terribly sorry—that shouldn't be happening. Please come back over to the back wash."

After carefully removing the pink from her hair and applying the correct toner, I make a mental note to never to ask some else to mix my colours for me. I am now running over an hour behind. Clients start to complain. I've never felt so stressed. Thankfully the day finally ends. I am cleaning up my station when Rebecca calls me into her office.

"Bella, can you come in here please?" she says, and I instantly have a bad feeling about this.

"Come in, close the door behind you, and take a seat please."

I sit down facing Rebecca.

"Right, I will cut to the chase. I have had numerous complaints about you this last week from clients and staff. Your head obviously isn't in your work anymore. I took a chance on you, Bella, and until this past week, you have been just what the salon needed. Foster & Thomas has already boosted your career and will continue to do so as long as you get your head back into your work. I am assuming your personal life has changed and this is what is distracting you. I suggest that you have good think about what is important—is it your career, which could be made or ended here? Or a boyfriend who will probably drop you like he has all his previous others?"

"Rebecca, I...."

"No, Bella—I do not want to hear any excuses. The decision is yours. I'm not back in the salon now until next week. I'm trusting you'll make the right decision, and I will see you then."

Rebecca stands, picks up her bag, and exits the room, leaving me absolutely gobsmacked. Did she just tell me to break up with Damien or I will lose my job? What the hell. After the week I have had, I can't stop the tears that pour from my eyes and the sob in my chest as I catch my breath. How the heck does she even know about Damien? Something doesn't feel right. I need to get out of here.

I'm getting my things from the staff room just as Mike walks in.

"Hey, Bella—is everything okay?" he asks.

"Fine, Mike, thanks. I just need to get home." I rush out, not making eye contact with anyone. Rebecca said she had complaints from members of staff too. I can't think who I have upset.

When I get to my room, I climb into bed fully clothed. I text Damien and say I'm not feeling well, so I can't see him tonight. He keeps ringing me, but I decline the calls. I can't speak to him right now. I don't want to speak to anyone. I just want to sleep. It's been such a stressful week, and I am mentally and physically drained. It doesn't take long me to fall into a deep sleep.

During the early hours, I wake up with the feeling that someone is watching me. Lying really still, I listen for any sound. But I don't hear anything—maybe I am imagining it. I try and go back to sleep, but the sense of being watched is overwhelming. It's funny how a human's senses work. We don't always trust them, but we should. My dad always told me to trust my instincts. He said that all creatures' instincts have been developed over millions of years. Animals are born and follow their instincts to survive, and we as humans should do the same.

I open my eyes and scan the room without moving. It's dark, but I can make out the room and furniture. I got into bed in such a hurry last night that I didn't shut the curtains, so there's a little moonlight coming in from outside. I look out into the window, and I see the reflection of the room. Something catches my eye. It's the shape of a figure—a large—probably male—figure. They aren't moving. They're just standing there. Watching me. My heart starts to beat hard and fast. I try to control my breathing so as not to make any noise.

What the hell do I do? My phone's on the bedside table. I could grab that, but it will be of no use if this guy wants to hurt me. My bedside light is a metal sculpture. I've never liked it, but now I couldn't happier that it's beside my bed. It will definitely do some damage and give me some form of chance, I hope. I lie there for another minute and build up my courage. Screaming would be pointless; these walls are pretty much soundproof. I'll get up, hit them with it, run to the door, and go to Katie's room or bang on as many doors in the hallway as I can.

Okay, I'm ready.

As quickly as I can, I sit up, grab the lamp, and jump to my feet beside the bed, ripping the plug out of the wall as I do.

"Bella! It's me! It's me, Damien. It's okay—calm down."

But I don't hear him. He is coming closer to me. My adrenaline has taken over, and I throw the lamp in his direction. It takes some force, as it is so heavy. Damien, however, catches it as if it weighs nothing and sets it down on the bed. "Bella, it's me."

I feel a wave of relief as the familiar voice

finally registers. He pulls me into him and wraps his arms around me. I'm shaking as my body calms down from the shock.

"I'm so sorry, my Bella—I had to see you. I didn't mean to scare you. I had to make sure you were okay. You weren't answering my calls."

"My God, Damien—you nearly gave me a heart attack," I say breathlessly.

"That was not my intention. Please forgive me."

He picks me up and puts me on the bed. He then gets the bedside lamp, plugs it back in, and switches it on. There he stands in his fitted blue jeans and skintight T-shirt. My eyes roam his body, and I'm instantly warmed from the inside. His dark eyes, however, are full of concern.

"What's the matter, Bella? You must tell me. I know there is something going on."

I don't want to tell Damien about what Rebecca has said—not yet, anyway. I need to work this out on my own. I know what Damien's reaction would be.

"I've had a terrible week at work—everything has just got on top of me. I just needed to some time to process it all."

Damien sighs and kisses the top of my head. I sense he doesn't quite believe me, but he doesn't question me any further.

"You work too hard. You need some time off. Come away with me? I need to go to New York tomorrow for a couple of days, as I have some business that needs to be handled face to face. It won't take long, and then we can spend the rest of the day together. I could extend the trip, and we could stay the week. What do you think?"

As much as a break sounds amazing and New York is a city I have always wanted to go to, I just can't go anywhere now. I need to sort out this mess with work, and the show is only a week away. I feel like I still have so much to do.

"As wonderful as that sounds, Damien, I really can't—now is just not a good time. Another time, though?" I ask hopefully.

"Okay, another time," he replies, getting onto the bed and pulling me along with him. He puts his face in my hair and inhales. "I've missed you, Bella. I needed to smell you, to touch you." He brings his hand to my face and turns it to his. He kisses me slowly and gently, saying, "To taste you."

He then kisses me with such passion and possessiveness, the tingles run through me, warming and bringing that special place in between my legs alive. "I need you, Bella. You're mine. Please do not hide from me again. Whatever the reason, you must come to me."

"I'm sorry, I should have explained. I've missed you too."

His dominating and primal ways should scare me, but they no longer do. I just melt in his arms. I feel so safe with him. I literally surrender my whole body to him. He can take me and have me any way he wants… and he does.

Chapter 14

Bella

I wake in the morning feeling empowered. A gorgeous, intelligent, and powerful man spent all night worshipping every inch of my body.

I decide I'm not going to let Rebecca get to me. I am damn good at my job, and I'm not going to be pushed around. Damien walks in from the bathroom. He's wearing a black suit that fits him perfectly. He's freshly shaven, his hair is styled the way I've shown him how to do it, and he smells amazing.

"Good morning, my beautiful Bella. How are you feeling this morning?" he asks.

"I'm feeling wonderful. You were just what I needed last night. I'm sorry I didn't ring you."

The conversation with Rebecca runs through my head. The way she spoke about my "boyfriend" and how he would "drop me" has infuriated me. How dare she. "Damien, do you know Rebecca, my manager? Other than as my manager, I mean?"

Damien comes over and sits beside me on the bed. "No, not that I know of. Why do you ask?"

"She said something to me after work last night; she basically said that having a boyfriend was affecting my work," I explain.

"That's ridiculous. Is this why you were so upset?" Damien asks as he tucks my hair behind my ear and looks deeply into my eyes. "I don't think we've been as discreet as we thought. It's time we let our relationship go public, Bella. I want the world to know you're mine. What do you think?" Damien smiles at me with a hopeful look on his face.

He makes me happy—he makes me *really* happy. I think I'm okay with people knowing about us now. I know some people will have their opinions on our relationship, but I think I can handle it. We can't stay secret forever.

"Yes, lets tell everyone." I agree excitedly. "But I need to tell my parents first,"

"All right. Would you like me to be with you when you do?"

"No, I'll call them and tell them today—then they'll be at the show on Saturday night. You can meet them then. You're still coming, aren't you?" I ask.

"I wouldn't miss it for the world. I'm leaving for New York today, but I plan to be back on Wednesday evening. As soon as business is taken care of, I will be on the plane back to you. And on that note, I need to go." He pulls me in and gives me a passionate loving kiss, melting me the way he always does. "I hate to leave you, but I must. Until

Wednesday, my Bella."

"I look forward to it. Ring me when you get there," I say.

He smiles, nods, and leaves my apartment. I flop back down into my bed. It's Sunday, and I have nowhere to be. I'm lovingly knackered, so here is where I will be staying. I snuggle up, smelling Damien on my pillow. I close my eyes and fall sleep with a smile on my face.

I spend the morning in bed, just like I planned. I ring my parents and tell them about Damien. Well, I don't tell them everything, but enough to ensure they are happy for me and looking forward to meeting him on Saturday. After that, I go out for food and a few drinks with Katie, then ring Chloe and catch up on what has been going on. The girls make me feel much better about my bad week last week and run-in with Rebecca.

I am just about to go to bed when my phone rings. It's Tiffany.

"Hey, hon, I really need your help." Tiffany sounds a little panicked. "It's a hair emergency. Can you come to my apartment and bring your kit please?" she pleads.

"Yeah, sure. I'm on my way." I get my kit and make my way down to Tiffany. I wonder what has happened? She normally comes into the salon for her hair.

Tiffany opens the door with a towel around her head.

"Oh, thank you, Bella." She pulls me inside with a hug. "It's a nightmare! I've got chewing gum in my hair! I tried to comb it out, but it just spread all the way down. So, I thought I could wash it out. But the warm water melted the gum, and now it's even worse," she says with sob. "I'm working tonight, and I've a meeting with my new manager. I am sure she doesn't like me, so I can't turn up like this." Tiffany sits on her sofa with her head in her hands.

"Don't worry," I reassure her. "I'll have it sorted in no time. I just need something that isn't in my kit—peanut butter. I'll be back in five."

"Peanut butter?" she repeats, sounding surprised.

"Yep, I promise we will have that gum out in a jiffy."

When I return, I take the towel off her head and assess the damage. She's made a mess. I section the hair where I can, apply the peanut butter, and start to comb the hair, working my way up.

"Did they teach you this in college, then? Peanut butter gets out chewing gum?"

I laugh. "No, my mum did, actually. I came home with gum or Silly Putty in my hair a few times as kid. Anything oil based will remove it, really. That, and a large-tooth comb. So anyway. How exactly did you get chewing gum in your hair?"

"Well, I was with this guy last night.

Another one who I will not be seeing again. And well, we were, you know, in bed. When we started, he had gum in his mouth. It was an Airwaves one, you know, the really minty ones. They're good for when you're, you know.... Makes it more sensitive. Anyway, when we finished, the gum was no longer in his mouth—it was in my hair!"

I burst out laughing. Thankfully Tiffany laughs too. Why do things like this always happen to her? I manage to get all the gum out, and then I wash and dry her hair. Tiffany gets off to work on time, and I finally get to bed.

Monday is my last day off before the show on Saturday. I spend the whole day prepping. I have a couple of hours with my model. I'm doing two different styles—one down in waves with some accessories and one up. I know them both like the back of my hand, and my timing is perfect. I'll colour it on Friday so it's fresh for the show. For the rest of the day, I go over my presentation. I only have five minutes to speak about our looks, but a lot can be said in that amount of time. I don't want to be reading from anything. I'm incredibly nervous and anxious. I feel physically sick when I think about it, to the point where I don't want to do it. But I will.

This is something I have dreamed of doing my whole life. Me standing onstage, showcasing my work to the world. Well, not the world, but you know what I mean. I'm going to be fine, and I know I will love it when I'm actually doing it.

My phone rings, and Damien's name lights up my screen. I smile as I feel the little butterflies in my tummy.

Damien

Bella answers on the first ring. It's so good to hear her voice. I hate being so far away from her, especially since I know something is troubling her. Something happened at work. That Rebecca's got something to do with it. Bella sounds a lot happier today, excited about her show. But I can't help worrying.

I call Mike as soon as my call with Bella ends.

"Mike, what's the latest at the salon? Bella's had a bad week, and I want to know why."

Mike goes over the last week's events with me. There's something not right with all these incidents.

"Thanks, Mike. Keep me updated."

Something is seriously off. I email IT and ask for a background check on Rebecca. I want to know everything, and I know they'll find it.

The King Security offices are based out of the top three floors of a high-rise building in Lower Manhattan. I'm greeted by the doorman and receptionist.

"Good morning, Mr. King." I nod in response. I don't do small talk.

I enter the private lift using my security

card. It feels a lifetime since I was last here. I used to spend twelve hours a day, six days a week here until my father died. I'm not sure if it's his passing or meeting Bella, but I'm looking at life a whole lot differently now.

The lift chimes, bringing me out of my thoughts of Bella. The doors open, and I walk out onto the top floor. Penny is already here, talking to my office PA.

"Good morning, Mr. King," they say in unison.

"I've left the documents for your meeting on your desk, and Josh is in your office waiting for you," Penny explains.

"Good morning ladies, and thank you Penny." I greet as pass them and head to my office.

Josh and I run through the itinerary of the meeting. We have taken on some new clients that King Security has been declining to represent for many years. Against my better judgment, however, Josh has persuaded me to take them on. The company are... let's just say not always legal, which is why I have been so against our collaboration. However, Josh has assured me that we won't be brought into anything illegal. This is why I'm here, and so is Mr. Davis, my lawyer, along with a couple of his team.

Our new clients are shown into our office.

"Mr. Graves, please come in. Take a seat," I say.

Mr. Graves is followed in by two very large

men. They both resemble Lurch from the Addams family. They may look scary to some, but not to Josh and me. Mr. Graves is the owner of a family-run loan shark and debt collecting business. The "business" has been going for generations. Over the years, it has become "less ethical" in the words of Mr. Graves, which has resulted in family members being seriously hurt and killed. Mr. Graves wants our expertise to help bring the business back to moral ground.

"Mr. King, I know your reputation and you know mine. We are both very respected in our worlds. I can't thank you enough for meeting with me today. You are my only hope of stopping any further tragedies in my family. If there is anything I can do to repay the favour, you just say the word."

"That won't be necessary, Mr. Graves. Plus, we haven't signed the contract yet," I say sternly.

The meeting continues well into the evening, and by the time I get back to my apartment, I can hardly keep my eyes open. My first thought when I walk through my home is how lonely it feels. Considering I have lived here for ten years, it's strange that I feel so homesick. The apartment is furnished with premium furniture. I had an interior designer do a full renovation only twelve months ago. It just goes to show, it's not what's in a house that makes it a home, it's who. It has been a while since I was here, and I realise this has never really felt like home. I only slept, ate, and worked here.

Bella comes into my mind. My Bella. Could there be a more perfect name for such a beauty? I instantly smile at the thought of her. Now, *she* makes me feel like I'm at home. I pull out my phone to ring her—her voice is just what need. I look at the time. It's 4:00 a.m. in the UK. No wonder I'm tired. I got straight off the plane and went to the office. It's too late to ring my Bella now, but I see she has left me some voice notes on WhatsApp. I strip off and climb into bed. I listen to her good-night messages and send her one back. I can hear the smile in her voice when she speaks to me, and it makes me smile too. Chuckling to myself, I wonder what the hell has happened to me. I'm pining over a woman. This isn't me—well, it didn't used to be me, but I like it.

Bella

"Hey, Bella."

It's Tiffany. She comes running into the salon with a huge box in her hands that says Flower Company on it. "This is for you—they dropped them off at reception a while ago, and I was so busy, I completely forgot to bring them up. Anyway, I must get back, as the phone's been ringing off the hook all morning. And thanks again for last night—I owe you one!"

"Thanks, Tiff, and don't mention it—I am glad I could help," I shout back as she runs out of the salon as fast as she can in her three-inch stiletto heels. I carry the delivery into the staffroom and open the box. Inside there are twelve… what I think *were* red roses, but they are completely dead now. The petals are almost black and completely wilted.

"Hey, what you got there, kid?"

It's Mike. He makes me jump as he towers behind me, staring over my shoulder at the flowers. "Is it me, or do they look a bit dead?" Mike asks as he scratches his head.

"Yeah," I chuckle. "Tiffany said they'd been delivered a while ago and she forgot to bring them up."

"I think it was more than a while ago. Is there a card? Who are they from?" Mike asks.

"I can't see one. I think I know who they're from, though."

I wonder when he sent them? I bet Damien thinks I'm so ungrateful, not thanking him for the flowers. I'll speak to him later and explain. There's no saving them, unfortunately, so I put them in the bin and get to work on my next client. The day passes with no complications, thank goodness. I don't wish to repeat last week ever again.

When I get back to my apartment after work, I feel a strange sensation like someone's been in my room. I switch all the lights on and have a good look around. There's no one here, and I can't see anything missing. I'm so exhausted, my mind is playing tricks on me.

I get into bed and call Damien.

"Good evening, Bella."

He's smiling as he speaks. I can hear it in his voice; he sounds happy to hear from me. That makes me happy too.

"Hi, how are you? How did your meeting go?" I ask.

"As well as could be expected. We've signed the contracts, so I will be flying back to England tomorrow," he replies.

"That's great news, Damien. I have missed you."

"And I you, Bella. I've missed every delicious bit of you."

"I can't wait to see you." I blush thinking of how he devours me. I still can't believe this handsome, powerful, kind man is in a relationship with little old me. If it is all a dream, I hope I never wake up. We talk for an hour so until Damien really must go. I'm soon falling asleep with a smile on my face.

Today is Wednesday. Damien is home tonight. He's asked me to be at his apartment when he gets home. I'm going to surprise him with a home-cooked meal. He mentioned to me recently that he really missed his mum's cooking and that he's never really been a fan of the fancy food at restaurants. My mum has always been a good cook, too—traditional English dishes, mainly. I have so many fond memories of us baking and cooking together. Reminiscing makes me feel a little homesick. Still, I'll see my parents on Saturday, and I'll make sure to plan a visit home soon.

I have decided to make a cottage pie, as I know I make a good one. It's my mum's recipe, and it's easy and quick, which is what I need. My day at work is busy. I have boring clients who don't want to talk to me, so I make mental notes on what I need to do, where I need to go, and what I need to get when I finish work.

"Delivery for Bella White?"

There's a guy at the door of the salon, shouting over Mike. Mike is trying to take the parcel from the delivery guy, but he doesn't want to give it to him. Mike must breathe in or something, because his shoulders go up about five inches and his body gets wider. He says something else to the guy that I can't make out, as it just sounds like a growl. The guy lets go of the parcel and quickly disappears.

"I'll just put this away in the staffroom for you, Bella," Mike says with a wink as he walks past me.

I really like Mike. He's like a big, lovable grizzly bear. He's in his late forties, I'd guess. I suddenly realise I don't know much about him, really. I make a mental note to get to know him better.

When finally I finish my last client, I go to the staffroom and collect my things, but I don't see my parcel. "Hey, Mike? Where did you put my parcel?"

Mike walks in the staffroom, looking a bit sheepish.

"Well, Bella, I'm very sorry to tell you this, but Damien sent you a cake, and I was hungry, so I ate it. Sorry."

"Oh, Mike, what are you like," I say with a laugh and slap his chest playfully. "Well, I've got to go—I've loads to do, so I need to get going. I'll see you tomorrow, though, and I'd better have another cake!"

Mike laughs, and then I'm out of there. There's a lovely little farm shop around the corner I want to get my ingredients from before it closes.

With my heavy bags of shopping, I let myself into Damien's apartment. I've been here many times, but it still excites me when I enter. I carry my bags into the kitchen and put them on the island. I smile to myself as I remember my first encounter with it. I look through the many cupboards to find the equipment I need. This kitchen has absolutely everything, and it all looks brand new.

I find a frying pan, a saucepan for the potatoes, and a large glass Pyrex dish. I wash my hands and get started. I begin by peeling and cutting the potatoes then dicing the onion and carrots. I brown off the mince beef and combine the diced carrot and onion with it. I add the beef stock and season with salt and pepper. I leave it to simmer and the potatoes to boil.

While it's simmering, I run myself a bath. Damien's not due home for a while, so a relax in his huge jacuzzi tub sounds like a perfect idea. Plus, I want to smell all fresh just in case Damien is hungry for a little more than cottage pie. I laugh to myself—he's turning me into a sex maniac. Never before have I had these thoughts, but I'm not complaining.

I mash and whisk the potatoes with salted butter. I add the mince mixture into the casserole dish and place the potatoes on top. A generous sprinkle of cheddar cheese over it, and it's in the oven on a medium heat. Perfect. I quickly wash up and get in the bath.

Chapter 15

Damien

My phone rings as I step off the plane.

"Mike. What's happened now?!" I demand.

"Bella received a flower delivery yesterday, but the flowers were dead. Tiffany brought them up, saying she had meant to bring them up earlier but had been too busy. When Bella opened them, we assumed they were from you and that Tiffany had them for weeks. But last night, I couldn't stop thinking about it. It just felt odd. I asked Tiff, and she said they'd only been delivered that day but earlier in the morning."

I have a bad feeling about this.

"Have you rung the company that sent the flowers?" I ask.

"Yeah, I rang the flower company, and they said the order was specifically for dead roses. They were paid for in cash by a male but could give no description."

"Okay. Can you pass this information on to Josh? See if he can find out more. Thanks, Mike, and if there's anything else, ring me straight away."

"Well, actually, boss, another parcel arrived

at the salon today. Bella was busy, and I made sure I took it from the delivery guy. He had apparently been given strict instructions to only give it to Bella. Obviously, I didn't let that happen. Anyway, inside the parcel was a heart."

What?

"A heart? What sort of heart? Like, a heart-shaped cushion?" I ask.

"No, a real heart, boss. A pig's heart, actually. I traced it back to a butcher downtown. Someone went in and paid over the odds for it to be delivered to Bella. They paid cash, but again, no one could give me a description. Sorry, boss."

"Did Bella see any of this?"

"Well, that's the other thing—she saw me accepting the parcel and then asked where it was. I told her it was cake from you and that I ate it," he explains.

"A cake from me?"

"Yeah, boss. She thinks the flowers were from you, so it was the first thing I thought of."

"Okay, Mike. I appreciate everything you've done. Ring Josh for me now and tell him everything you've just told me."

"Will do."

My blood boils as my brain goes over the people who would want to do this to Bella. Could it be Pete or John? I will get to the bottom of it. But for now, I need to see my woman.

The smell as I walk into my apartment back

in England takes my breath away. It's a mixture of Bella's sweet and fresh aroma and home-cooked food. I can't remember the last time I came home to such a welcome. I walk into the kitchen and see Bella dancing about while dishing out dinner. She's wearing her pjs—little pink shorts and a white vest top. Her hips are moving to the beat of the music. Her back is to me, and her wavy golden-blonde hair is swishing along with her body. This, here, is what I want to come home to every day. I feel the strangest tightness and heaviness in my chest. Is this what home is? Is this what love feels like?

Bella turns and looks at me with those beautiful blue eyes—her smile is big and genuine when she sees me. The alpha in me wants to walk over there, pick her up, and carry her straight into my bedroom. I don't, though, as it looks like she has gone to a lot of trouble. The food smells amazing, and my stomach growls in anticipation. The man in my trousers will have to wait. But not for long.

I put down my coat and case and go to my Bella. Without saying a word, we wrap our arms around each other and kiss like our lives depend on it. Through our lips, we pass feelings of longing and appreciation for finally being together again.

Bella breaks the kiss. "Well, hello, Mr. King, I have missed you terribly," she says with a sultry look in her eyes.

"Grrr, and I you, Bella. It's taking all my strength not to throw you over my shoulder and carry you into that bedroom."

Bella giggles as she blushes. "Hold that thought, handsome. First, we eat. Take a seat, and I'll bring it over."

I sit at the island. There's a bottle of wine and two glasses set out. I open it and pour. Bella brings over our plates, and I am overwhelmed with emotion. It's cottage pie... and it's my absolute favourite. My mum used to make it for me all the time. I haven't eaten it since she died, and I haven't wanted to. But today, I can't think of anything I would rather eat here and now with Bella.

"Is everything okay, Damien? Do you not like cottage pie?"

She must be able to see the emotion in my eyes.

"I know it's not very exciting, but I remember you said you missed home-cooked food? This is one of my favourites, so I thought it would be nice for change."

"It's perfect, Bella."

She wraps her arms around my shoulders, giving me a little squeeze, and kisses the top of my head before sitting down next to me. We sit in silence for a few minutes, eating the delicious homemade meal and drinking our wine. I have never felt happier and more at home.

Once we have started to satisfy our appetites, we each talk about our day. Bella apologises on behalf of Tiffany and Mike for ruining my gifts and says she can't thank me enough for my thoughtful gestures. I wish to God they were from me.

My mind is in overdrive, and I'm furious with whoever is sending these things to Bella. They obviously want to upset her, and this makes me sick with anger. I will kill anyone that even tries to hurt a hair on her head. I try and keep myself neutral. I don't want to lie to Bella, but her worrying will only make things worse. I don't know what their endgame is, but I'm going to find out.

Bella stands up and takes our empty plates to the dishwasher. She bends over to load the plates in the bottom drawer. Her short pjs rise up as she does so, exposing her perfection of a backside. That's all I need. I am on my feet and behind her in an instant. She giggles and stands up at my presence. I spin her around, pick her up, and throw her over my shoulder. I slap her bottom, and she lets out a playful scream.

"Put me down, Damien." She laughs and wriggles.

I march us into my bedroom, the lights turn on, and I throw her onto the bed.

"Lights two!" I command.

Bella lies on her back, holding herself up on her elbows. I stand at the foot of the bed. She's perfect. So naturally beautiful. Her blue eyes hold mine, her cheeks flushed a little pink. Her tongue flicks out and wets her plump lips. I loosen my tie and throw it to the floor. I unbutton my shirt and dispose of it in the same way.

"Undress for me, Bella." I instruct.

Bella takes in my chest. Then her eyes roam down to my pants, and she notices my growing arousal trying to escape. Her eyes visibly light up, which adds to the urgent need to free myself. Bella pulls her top over her head and slips off her shorts, and then she throws them at me with a giggle. I catch them and burrow my face into them. I inhale while keeping eye contact with her. I think her arousal just stepped up a notch.

"Lie back and open your legs."

Bella does as I say. With her back flat on the bed and her knees bent, she opens wide for me. There she is in all her glory, glistening and ready for me—only me. My Bella.

Bella

It's 5:00 a.m. on Saturday, the day of the hair show. I'm sat up in bed, and my anxiety is through the roof. I didn't sleep a wink last night. I have this terrible feeling something bad is going to happen, but I know it's just my mind playing tricks on me.

I try not listening to my anxious thoughts and concentrate on my positive ones. I'm completely prepared, if not overprepared. I know my presentation off by heart, and I have planned for every mishap. I have an emergency model if something should happen to my original. My plan-B model is my bestie Chloe, who is travelling down with my parents this morning. I have everything written down and stuck to the back of a colour chart in case my mind goes blank and I forget everything. I have two of all my tools and equipment. I have thought of every worst-case scenario and planned for it. It is going to be fine, I tell myself. I coloured my model's hair yesterday. We had a full dress-rehearsal last night, and everything went smoothly.

I may as well get up, I think to myself. *I'm not going to get to sleep now, and lying here thinking things over is making me worse.* The salon is closed today so we can prepare for tonight. I'm completely organised and I just need to get myself ready, but it is too early for that. I slept at Damien's last night, and I'm glad I am here. I think I would be freaking out even more if I was on my own. Damien breathing throughout the night kept me sane. I quietly get up out of bed.

Damien sits bolt upright. "Bella, where are you going?" There's no sneaking past him.

"I can't sleep, so I thought I'd get up and make a drink," I whisper.

"I'll come with you."

"No. really, I'm fine—you go back to sleep," I insist.

"No, I'm up. Come on, I'll make us some coffee." Damien puts his arm around me and gives me a little squeeze. He knows I'm freaking out.

Damien distracts me all morning. He fills me with confidence and makes me feel so much better.

He really is a remarkable man.

My parents and Chloe are due to arrive any minute. Damien and I are waiting at the front of the hotel to meet them. Damien has arranged for George to pick them up from Euston train station in the limo. He insisted, in true Damien form, so I couldn't refuse. Plus, my mum and Chloe will have loved it. I also can't imagine my dad catching the tube, so I am very grateful.

I have butterflies, and I'm giddy with anticipation. I'm so excited to see my parents and Chloe and I can't wait for my parents to meet Damien. I hope they like him. I start to get a little panicky—what if they don't like him? He is a bit older than me, and he's a very strong man in physical ability and personality.

Oh God.

Damien squeezes my hand and pulls me in for a hug. He takes a deep breath, smelling my hair. I love it when he does this.

He tilts my face up to his and looks me in the eyes. "Everything is going to be fine. I'll be on my best behaviour, I promise." He smiles his handsome smile and kisses me on my lips. It is all I need to settle my nerves, and it's just in time, as the limo pulls up in front of us.

George gets out and opens the back door. Chloe jumps out with an excited scream. "Bella!!" Chloe dances over to me and gives me the biggest hug. She kisses me all over my face, making me giggle. "I've missed you so much, and I'm so excited for tonight—eeek!"

She lets go of me and throws her arms around Damien, much to his surprise. Damien is not an affectionate man and doesn't show his feelings (well, apart from in the bedroom). He hates this sort of thing, but he takes it well, bless him.

He taps Chloe on the back and releases her arms from around his neck. "It's nice to see you again, too, Chloe," he says with grin.

I look back at the limo, and out steps my mum with the help of my dad.

"Mum!" I make my way over and hug them both. Tears fill my eyes, and I'm overwhelmed with emotion.

"Hey, come on, petal," says my dad.

"I'm just so happy to see you."

"And we you, sweetheart."

We have another moment, and then I walk them over to Damien.

"Mum, Dad, this is Damien. Damien, these are my parents, Olivia and Henry White."

There's a look on Damien's face I have never seen before; he looks nervous. I smile—he really cares what they think of him. This big, powerful, handsome, billionaire man respects the opinions of little old Henry and Olivia White. My love for this man grows that bit more. Damien puts out his hand to my dad. My dad takes it, they shake strongly, and then Damien shakes my mum's.

"Mr. White, Mrs. White. It is my pleasure to meet you both," he says.

"The pleasure is all ours, Damien. Bella hasn't told us too much about you, but we can tell you are making her happy, and that's all we can ask." My mum beams at him seemingly already impressed by him.

Damien seems to relax a little at that.

"And while we are here, we can get to know you for ourselves, can't we?" says my dad. I know he's going to be on guard. Especially after John, whom I know he partly blames himself for.

"You can indeed Mr. White." Damien agrees.

We walk into the hotel through the revolving doors and are greeted with the now-familiar sweet smell of King.

"Wow, what a beautiful hotel. Gosh, Henry, do you smell that? It's the most beautiful scent," my mum says, taking a deep breath in.

"Aye, I do *love*.. Very nice indeed," he replies.

Damien smiles to himself. He loves when people comment on the signature scent, as it reminds him of his mother.

"Mr. King, your guests' rooms are ready. Shall I take their luggage to their rooms and get them settled?" a member of staff asks Damien.

I see my dad's eyebrows rise, and his brain must be starting to tick over. I have told my parents Damien's full name, but I have not actually told them that he owns the hotel (well, the chain), but I think the penny may have just dropped for my dad. My mum, on the other hand, is oblivious; she's excitedly looking around the hotel and pointing things out to my dad.

"Mr. and Mrs. White, Harry here will take your luggage and show you to your room," says Damien.

"Please, Damien, call us Olivia and Henry," my mum quickly says.

"Mr. White is fine with me," my dad says, half joking, half serious.

"Henry! He's just joking—ignore him." My mum laughs and smacks my dad on the chest, giving him "the look."

"Once you're settled, maybe you could meet us in the bar and get some lunch. I've another couple of hours before I need to get ready," I say.

"Lovely, sweetheart—yes. See you in a few," my mum replies.

They walk off, following Harry to the lifts.

"Hey, Hazzer?! Chuck this in Bella's room on your way, will you. Cheers, cock," shouts Chloe while she throws her bag at Harry. Good job he can catch.

This gets a laugh from Damien. Chloe, she's a one. I've missed her.

She walks in between us, putting an arm around each of our necks. "So, who's buying me a drink?"

We all have lunch in the bar. It's so lovely having my favourite people all together and getting along. It's just what I need to take my mind

157

off tonight. I hardly touch my lunch, though, as I am so nervous. I just can't stomach anything. Damien's really making an effort with my parents, and he's kept my dad talking throughout.

"Yeah, I just got a new Callaway hybrid," my dad boasts. "You'll have to come up with Bella next time, and we can have a round at my club."

"I'd enjoy that, thank you," Damien replies.

Damien looks my way, and I give him the biggest smile. Damien doesn't play golf.

Chloe stands and gestures for me to get up. "Right, beautiful. We need to go and make you look even more beautiful. Let's go get ready. I need a wine, but I need to do my hair and makeup first, or else I'll look like a clown." Chloe pulls me up out of my chair.

"I'll see you later, Mum and Dad."

Damien gets up. "I'd better get going too. I will see you both this evening. I'll escort the girls back to Bella's apartment."

Damien walks us to the staff quarters, where a plump employee asks him, "Mr. King, can I have a word?"

"You go, babe. We need to get ready. I'll see you there, okay?" I say as he pulls me in and kisses me.

"See you there. Good luck, my Bella. You will be fabulous," he responds.

"What is it?" I hear Damien bark at the employee as he walks away. He's so grumpy and stern with everyone else. I like that I see a completely different side to Damien that no one else does.

Chloe and I get ready in my bedroom, dancing about to music. She does my makeup and I do our hair. Then we look at ourselves in the mirror.

"God, Bella, you look so hot!" Chloe says to me.

"You look amazing, too, Chloe."

My dress is one from the brand's collection. I do feel pretty good in it. I am a little worried about my shoes, though. They are very beautiful, silver and sparkly, but the heel is a little higher than I usually wear.

"Dutch courage." Chloe hands me a shot of sambuca.

We down them and clink glasses. I take a deep breath. I'm so ready for tonight now. It's going to be a night I'll never forget—I can feel it.

Chapter 16

Damien

I text Bella to wish her good luck.

Damien: Break a leg, my Bella. You will be wonderful. I will be with you every minute xx

Bella: Thank you. I feel sick. Xx

The King suite is filling up. People are beginning to take their seats. It's about ten minutes before the show starts. I've made sure security is tight tonight, putting more men on the event than I would normally have, but I have to be prepared for Bella. Everything seems to be going to plan. The room is dressed with white silk drapes. Large flower arrangements are everywhere. The space is lit up with pink and purple lights. Waiters and waitresses walk around with champagne and canapés. Everyone is well dressed in evening wear. There are quite a few well-known fashion designers and people in the know here, apparently. Whatever that means.

I've just had my ear chewed off by Chloe for about fifteen minutes as she pointed all the different people out. Thank goodness Josh turned up and saved me. There's definitely something going on between them. Then the music and atmosphere in the room changes, and people hurry to get seated. I stand to the side of stage, where it's darker. I have a good view of the stage here and the rest of the room without being obtrusive. Well, so I thought. Bella's parents are sitting a couple of rows down from where I'm standing. Bella's mum gives me an excited wave, so I discreetly wave back.

The show starts, and I'm engrossed from the beginning. The designer is an avid climate activist. Each range of clothing tells a different story, all the materials are recycled, and the items of clothing can be changed and made into different garments. There are dresses that are also tops and trousers. It's a very clever concept. The models put on a spectacular show.

The makeup artists and hair stylists now come onto the stage. My Bella steps up to address the audience; she's so incredibly beautiful. She is wearing a strapless white figure-hugging dress with feathers all around the bottom. This is also part of the collection, apparently. I remember Bella talking about it while she showered this morning. My mind wasn't fully on what she was saying but more on what she was doing. My goodness, she literally takes my breath away. I suddenly feel a wave of jealousy that everyone else in the room can see her beauty. I want to carry her out, take her to my bed, and spank her bottom for making me feel like this.

But then she starts to speak.

Bella explains how they have created the hair looks on the models tonight using alternative methods of styling to save on electricity and water and how they've been working with product companies and designing recyclable packaging for hair products while using more natural-based colouring products. They've designed tools like combs, brushes, and clips out of bamboo and wood. She demonstrates how these are actually better for your hair. Bella speaks so passionately and confidently. I'm so proud of her. I realise the whole room is silent and listening intently to every word she says.

"And so, it has been and honour and privilege to work with such a talented and caring designer. She has really opened my eyes to what is possible and how little things can make a huge difference in our future and our children's future. Please take a look at the products, which are available for you to try. I hope we have inspired you —please stay and enjoy the rest of evening. Good night."

The whole room erupts in cheers and applause. Damn, what a woman! Bella and the models retreat backstage. I stand there, still in awe of what I've just witnessed. My anxious, scared little Bella from this morning has just taken over this whole room.

Josh appears by my side.

"Hey, Damien. She did great! It was a good show," he says.

"She was incredible," I muse.

"So, I've just had today's report back from the private investigator I've had trailing Rebecca, Bella's manager."

Josh now has my full attention.

"You'll never guess who she's been to lunch with today?"

"Who?" I demand.

"Claire's brother. Pete"

FUCK!

"I NEED EYES ON BELLA NOW!" I radio through to everyone on the floor.

Then I make my way through the crowds of people as quickly as I can. I climb up on the stage and run to the back. It's dimly lit, and there's hardly anyone here, just a few models packing up their things. I dash frantically up and down, looking for Bella,

"Has anyone seen Bella White?!" I shout. but everyone just shakes their heads. I radio again. "WHY THE FUCK DOES NOT ONE OF YOU HAVE EYES ON BELLA!"

Then I address Josh specifically. "Josh, come in. I need video surveillance on Bella's last movements"

"Already on it," he replies.

My heart is hammering in my chest. *Where are you, Bella? SHIT!* I punch the wall putting a hole in the plasterboard. I rest my head in my hands and crouch to the floor, trying to regain control of myself; this is not going to help find Bella. I take two deep breaths and channel my anger into adrenaline. I stand up and see the fire escape. I open the door leading outside onto a metal staircase. It's raining and extremely windy. It's pitch-black outside. I strain to see out. I get a glimpse of something halfway down the staircase. I run down the extremely slippery stairs, trying not to fall.

It's a sparkly silver shoe. Bella's shoe.

"Damien, you there?"

It's Josh, but the radio crackles as his voice comes through. I'm losing signal outside. I have one last look around, praying to see something. I run to the bottom of the staircase. It's just a dark back alley with bins. The bins, however, are all bunched together as if they've been moved to make way for something. A car or small van perhaps? I can't see any tracks on the cobble road. It's too wet—the road is full of puddles. I run back up the stairs and inside.

"Josh, what have you got?" I radio.

"There's no CCTV backstage because of privacy. We've got Bella exiting the stage and going backstage. Two minutes after, the cameras on the fire escape pick up a male wearing what looks like a security uniform, carrying something over his shoulder wrapped in black. Halfway down the stairs, something light in colour falls from whatever he's carrying. I've got someone going there now to check it out."

"Don't bother—it's Bella's shoe," I say.

"Right. There is a small van parked at the bottom of the stairs. He puts what he's carrying in the back and drives off. There's no movement at all from whatever he carried, Damien," Josh informs me.

"It's Bella, Josh, I know it. We need to find her."

"We will. Get back out and down that fire escape, and I will meet you on the road. The footage is being sent to you now."

Back outside, I search for anything that might lead me to Bella. But there's nothing. Whatever was there has been washed away with the rain. When I reach the end of the alley, I look up and down the road. Which way would they go? Where are they taking her? My heart constricts in my chest. Why wasn't she moving? Why didn't she fight? *Please be okay, Bella.* I say a silent prayer and vow to do everything to find her.

Josh pulls up at speed. The passenger door opens, and I get in.

"We've got traffic camera footage showing the vehicle turn right and head north," Josh begins. "I've got updates coming in as and when they get them. The only trouble is, we are two minutes thirty-five seconds behind them. Bella's phone has been found in the dressing area backstage. Mike's going through it to see if there's any indication as to who or where they are." His radio beeps. "Go ahead. I have Damien with me also."

"The vehicle has entered a multistorey car park and hasn't left. It arrived one minute ago, and you are about one minute to two minutes away. I have sent the location to your car."

The sat nav beeps, registering its destination.

"Floor it, Josh," I instruct, and Josh drives as quickly as he can in London city traffic, beeping for cars to move and mounting pavements to get round waiting taxis Its only minutes until we get there but it feels like hours.

We enter the car park which has five floors. We drive round each floor at speed. The car wheels skid and brakes screech, echoing through the building as we turn round to go up the slope to the next level. We reach the top level, but there are hardly any vehicles up here. A couple of cars and a dark blue van parked at the end in a shadowy corner. Josh drives to it. I am out of the car before he stops. The back doors are open. It's empty apart from a blanket and something sparkling in the back—Bella's other shoe.

"They've switched transport." I hear Josh radio through to surveillance.

I frantically look through the car to find any sort of clue as to where they may have taken her. Nothing. I get out my phone and make a call.

They answer on the first ring. "Mr. King, what can I do for you?" the familiar voice inquires.

"Mr. Graves, you said when I last saw you

that if there was anything you could do for me, I should ask. Well, I need a gun, and I need it urgently."

"Mr. King, I would have thought a man in your line of work and with your reputation would already own a gun?" he responds.

"I own many guns, Mr. Graves, but they are all either in New York or registered in my name. I need an unregistered gun one that cannot be traced back to me."

He understands immediately. "Let me make a call, and I will text you the address to it collect from." The call ends.

I never would have thought in a million years I would be taking Mr. Graves up on his offer of help. But needs must. He will be able to get me what I need much quicker than any other contact I have.

Back in the car, Josh finishes on the phone and turns to me. "I've got a team looking at all the vehicles which have exited the car park since this van drove in. There's twenty-four altogether. I've got someone bringing in Rebecca and a team looking for Claire's brother and his associates. I had Chloe on, hysterical, and Bella's father demanding answers. I've managed to put them off for a while, but you're going to have to speak to them soon. What do you want to do now? It's your call."

"Before I speak to anyone, I need answers. Take me to Rebecca," I reply.

We pull into the empty car park of our new London office. We've only just signed the lease, so the building is completely empty. Some of our team have taken her inside already. My blood boils as I get out of the car and enter the building. I need answers, and she is going to give them to me. As I walk down the hallway, I can hear Rebecca shouting.

"Why am I here!? This is kidnap, you know. I'll have you all arrested, or worse. I demand you let me go!" Rebecca is sitting at a table. Mike and James from my team are pressing firmly on her shoulders, preventing her from getting up.

"Guys, thank you. I will take it from here," I say. Whichever way this goes, I don't want them being involved.

They exit the room, and Rebecca stands up.

"SIT THE HELL DOWN!!!" I shout as I boot one of the chairs next to her. It flies across the room, smashing the window.

The colour drains from Rebecca's face, and she sits down. Good. She knows I mean business.

"Where is Bella?!"

Rebecca looks me in the eyes, her expression a little confused, like that wasn't what she expected me to say.

"I'm... I'm not sure, but I expect she'll be still at the show?" she says.

Either she is a really good actress with an amazing poker face or she's telling the truth. I decide to switch approach.

"How well do you know Pete?"

She doesn't look as surprised at this question.

"Quite well. We have been dating for about six months."

"And are you aware how I know Peter?" I ask.

"Yes, you killed his sister."

Fury builds inside me, but I must hold it together for Bella. "Regardless of what he may think I have done, kidnapping an innocent young woman is absolutely ludicrous!"

Rebecca looks at me as if trying to read my face. I'm holding myself together by a thread. I'm getting nowhere. The more time goes on, the less chance I have of finding her and the more danger she is in. Everyone knows the first twenty-four hours are the most important.

"What's happened, Damien?" She looks concerned now.

"Bella has been kidnapped, and you'd better start talking because if anyone has hurt her, I will be holding you responsible!"

Fear fills Rebecca's face. "Peter wouldn't kidnap Bella. He wanted her to know the truth about you. He wanted her to leave you and go back to where she came from. He wanted to hurt you and to show you he could get to you. But this.... Peter wouldn't do this." She begins to cry.

"Then where is he, Rebecca? Where the hell

is Peter? And why weren't you at the show tonight? It's all very convenient."

"I swear to you, I had nothing to do with this. Yes, I've messed with things in the salon to drive Bella out. She's been stealing my clients, and everyone in the salon likes her better than me. She's been taking over! It's been like the Bella show ever since she arrived. She can't do anything wrong."

I stare at her for a moment, trying to read her. She does look shocked and upset

"I may wish I had never employed her, but I'm not evil. I would never hurt her."

"You're one messed-up woman, Rebecca. Why wouldn't you just sack her?" I ask, losing patience.

"What for? Like I said, she never did anything wrong. Everyone loves her. If I had got rid of Bella, everyone in that salon would hate me and probably leave. The event tonight was the Bella show once again. I couldn't bear to see it. That designer should have picked me, the manager of Foster & Thomas, as brand stylist and ambassador. Not someone on my payroll!"

Rebecca may be a jealous bitch, and I will definitely be dealing with her, but she knows nothing. I'm good at reading people, and she has just told me truth in a roundabout way. She doesn't know where Bella is. I need to rethink. I leave the office building and check my phone—fifteen missed calls and voicemails from Chloe. I take a deep breath. I wish I had some good news for her.

Chapter 17

Bella

I'm lying down and it's dark. Am I in bed? I can feel movement, so I can't be in bed. I try and move, but I'm incredibly weak. I wince as I shift my back. Pain in my neck shoots down my spine. It's sore, like it has been hit with something. I lie still for a moment, trying to wake up from this dream or nightmare, but I don't. My mind goes to the last thing I remember. I was at the show. I had delivered my speech and presentation. It went extremely well. I managed to hold my nerves, and I think I came across as pretty confident and passionate. The audience seemed engaged, and there was a standing ovation at the end.

I remember seeing Damien's face. He was to the side of the stage. His eyes didn't leave my face, and he looked so proud of me. I felt so special being up there onstage, having him and my family and friends supporting me. The show ended, and we all exited the stage at the back. I went into the dressing room. Nobody was in there, as everyone else went out to celebrate. But I just wanted a couple of minutes to myself. I was so overwhelmed. I sat at a dressing table and looked at myself in the mirror. I felt a rush of emotion. Relief it was over, satisfaction that I had gone out there and faced my fears, and gratitude that I have been able to do it and demonstrate my passion.

Tears filled my eyes. I had put my face in my hands to take some deep breaths when I heard someone walk up behind me. It was a man by the sound of his footsteps, even though it felt like he was trying to be quiet. I assumed it was Damien looking for me. I lifted my head up to greet him, but as I did, something covered my face. I then felt a sharp pain in the back of my neck. Heat flowed up into my head and down into my body until... nothing. That's all I remember before now.

I force my eyes open. It's dark—pitch-black. I try and sit up, but my hands are tied behind my back. They're fastened at the wrists with what feels like zip ties. They are extremely tight, and when I move, they seem to get tighter. My legs are also tied together at the ankles. I rise up but bang my head on something above. I'm trying to make out where I am. I'm moving. I feel like I'm in a car. *Oh my God. I'm in a boot. I am in the boot of a car.* Panic sets in. *I can't breathe. Oh my God. I... can't... breathe.*

I wake up again. I'm not sure how long I've been out. Maybe a few minutes, maybe an hour. I need to control my anxiety. I can do this. I do this all the time—most days, actually. Usually for things like catching the tube or speaking to people

I don't know, but still.

Right—deep breaths. Take deep breaths.

Okay, so my goal is to assess the situation and find a way to get out. Simple. Here's what I know—my wrists and ankles are fastened with zip ties. I remember seeing a TikTok video about how to get out of them. Unfortunately, I never watched it properly. I'm kicking myself for that now—well, I would be if my ankles weren't stuck together.

Right, I'm in a car boot. I've seen in movies when people are in a car boot, they push out the rear light and wave their hand through. Let's see if I can do that. My hands are behind my back, so I feel with my feet. They are bare, which helps in feeling my way around. I squeeze my toes through the carpet of the boot around the end of what I think is the rear of the car. It is filthy. I'm getting bits of dirt—and I dread to think what else—stuck in between my toes. I work my feet through the gaps in the carpet, and I feel wires. I follow these with my toes and think I feel the rear light. I feel around for a bit longer until I'm sure this is what I'm going to do. I push on the light with my feet. It won't budge. I keep trying, pushing and kicking it as much as I can, but I'm too weak and it's well and truly stuck in.

I begin to panic again.

Just breathe, Bella.

I need to do something. I cannot give up. I decide to have one more go. I'm going to use all my strength, bringing it from all of my body. I am going to kick, bang, push the light out with my feet. After three... two...one... *CRACK!*

The pain is excruciating. Something snapped in my heel and ankle. I throw up from the pain. I've not much in my stomach, since I was so nervous, I hardly ate all day. But everything that was in there is now next to my face in the boot. I can't cope. I drift back off into the darkness.

Damien

"Damien why haven't you been answering my calls?! Have you found Bella? Do you know where she is?!"

I ignore her questions.

"Chloe, have you any idea who would want to kidnap Bella or where she might be?"

"Yes!" she says.

Wait? What? That's not what I expected her answer to be.

"What do you mean yes?!" I ask.

"Well, I have an idea. I've been thinking, Damien, and I have a feeling it might be John. He's completely gone off the rails since Bella left him. He's been disappearing for days and weeks at a time. He doesn't speak to his friends or his parents. I've done some ringing around, and it turns out his grandma died a couple of months ago and left him her house. No one seems to know where the house is other than it's in the Lake District somewhere. I've tried to get hold of John's parents, but they're on a plane to Australia and don't land for another seventeen hours."

I'm annoyed with myself for not realising this sooner. I'm so used to everything that goes wrong in my life being a result of my actions with Claire.,

"Find out what flight they are on and get in contact with the airport they'll be able to contact the pilot. Speak to the police about this. They'll be able to help you. Let me know as soon as you find out anything else, even the slightest little detail. And thank you, Chloe."

I end the call and shout for Josh. "We're going to the Lake District!" With a quick stop, as Mr. Graves has sent me a location. We will collect the gun on the way.

I direct Josh to where the pin on the map is. I put on my gloves and get out of the car, my phone pings confirming I'm in the right place, next to a yellow grit box. Lifting the lid, I look inside, where there is a brown paper bag. I grab it and head back to the car.

Once I'm in the car, I get the gun out. I clean it, check it's loaded, and put it into my holster.

Josh has been watching me. "I think I know the answer to this, mate, but why aren't you using your own gun?"

"Because today I won't be using my gun to

wound and disarm, I shall be using it to kill."

Josh just nods.

It's going to take us around five hours to get to the Lake District from London. The Lake District is also 912 square miles in size, and we don't yet know where this house is. I hope to God my gut instinct is right and that is where she is. We are about two hours behind them now after all the messing about I've done. I should have rung Chloe sooner.

What has happened to my Bella? Bile threatens to release from my stomach. I mustn't let my feelings take over. I need to channel it into adrenaline and get the job done. Find Bella, kill the abductor, and bring Bella home.

The first two hours passed quickly, but now time is moving disturbingly slowly. I can't help my mind wandering to Bella and what she is going through. If he touches her...

"Argh!" I punch the dashboard in front of me in frustration. The air bag shoots out, slamming me back into my seat. "Shit!"

My anger rises. I fight with the air bag. I stab it with my pocketknife and push it back into the dash.

"Come on, Damien—channel it!" shouts Josh.

I've worked in many rescue situations like this, and I've never once lost my head. Then again, I have also never had to rescue my love before.

My love. It pains me to think that I still have yet to tell her this.

I knew I loved Bella from the start, but I wouldn't let myself admit it. My love for her is huge. My heart is pulled to hers when I'm not near her, and when she is in danger, like she is now, my heart physically hurts. I have heard people speak of agape love, but I thought it was fictional. I now know otherwise. I will kill whoever has her, even if I die trying.

Bella

The next time I wake up, I'm being carried by what feels like a strong male. I'm not sure if I'm dreaming, as it feels very familiar. I keep still and quiet. My foot is pulsating. I try and relax. I keep drifting in and out of consciousness. We are outside, and it's dark and cold. I'm not aware of the time, but it feels like the very early hours of the morning. I can hear the footsteps of the person carrying me. Their steps are heavy and make crunching noises in the crisp autumn leaves on the ground. We then enter a building of some sort.

I'm starting to wake up a lot more now, but my body is frozen in fear. I dare not move my body or open my eyes. It's taking all my strength just to breathe normally. The air smells damp and musty. We go through the building. It's very quiet and slightly warmer than outside, but not much. I feel as though I still have my dress on from the show and some kind of blanket is over me, but I'm still extremely cold. I begin to shiver uncontrollably. I try my best to keep still, but I can't.

I keep my eyes closed and say a silent prayer. *Please, can I go home? Please don't let him hurt me.*

I'm then laid down on what feels like a bed. I only just realise the zip ties which were around my wrists and ankles have been removed. Another blanket is placed over me, and he strokes my head. I'm still frozen in fear. I couldn't open my eyes if I wanted to. He hovers over me for what feels like minutes, and then he leaves the room. I hear the door being locked and a bolt slide across it.

I lie there, unable to move. I just try to get control of my breathing. I'm shaking so much, the bed is rattling. I don't want him to come back in, so I concentrate on slowing my breathing and stopping shaking. I decide to think of all the things that make me happy to try and take my mind off what is going on.

My mind first goes to Damien. God, Damien is going to be frantic when he realises I am missing. He must know I'm gone now. I wonder what he is doing at this moment in time. If I know Damien, he will have all his men out looking for me. I begin to worry about him. I hope he doesn't get hurt while trying to find me. Who knows who this man is and what he is capable of? That's if Damien can find me.

My heart sinks. *Let's not go there just yet.*

I lie there for a while, finding strength in thinking of my loved ones. I start to open my eyes. It is dark, but there's moonlight shining in between the curtains of a window. I push up onto my elbows and look around. I'm in a bedroom. There's a window to the right of me with tartan wool curtains. I'm lying on a wooden four-poster double bed. It has no drapes, just wooden posts. I push myself up a bit more. There is a wooden dressing table with a mirror against the wall opposite the end of the bed. To the left of that is a wooden door and on the left wall, a large wooden wardrobe. The furniture looks old but expensive and in good condition, from what I can make out in this light.

The room seems clean and tidy, although the air is stale and damp. I decide to get up and look through the window to see if I can escape. I bring my legs over the side of bed and put my feet on the floor. I stand up.

CRUNCH. "Ahh!" I forgot about my ankle. An agonising pain shoots up from my ankle into my brain. My ankle gives way, and my knees buckle with pain. I fall to the floor. I flip myself over to assess the damage. My right ankle is three times its usual size. The swelling goes all the way down to my toes and up to my knee it looks like my shin bone maybe broken too. Kicking the rear light definitely wasn't one of my best ideas. My ankle is bright red, bruising is starting to appear up my leg. My skin is tight and shiny. This doesn't look good, but it's the least of my worries right now, I suppose.

I pull myself up onto one leg, using the bed for support. I hop over to the window. I pull back the curtains and peer out. I'm on the ground floor. There's a wooden deck area outside the window, then a stone driveway, which is empty. All I see surrounding that are trees blowing in the wind. From here, I don't know where I'd go other than to run into the trees. And with this leg, I wouldn't get very far. I stand at the window for a minute, and I get the strangest déjà vu. I just have this weird feeling I have been here before. But I don't recognise anything.

I hop over to the bed and grab the blanket to wrap it around myself. I shuffle over to the dressing table and open the top drawer. It's full of underwear. MY UNDERWEAR. Wait—why? How is my underwear here? There's a set here I've not seen for weeks that I thought I had left at Damien's or had got lost in the laundry at the hotel.

I flop down on the edge of the bed. What the hell is going on? I stare at myself in the mirror on the dressing table. My makeup is practically all gone, apart from the dark shadows around my eyes from my mascara and eyeliner.

Then I spot something behind me in the mirror. On the wall above the bed is a painting of a house. It is a painting of this house.

Oh God, I know where I am.

Chapter 18

Bella

Shocked, I stay sat on the edge of the bed, staring at the painting through the mirror. I cannot believe my eyes. I then hear a bolt sliding across the door. The key turns in the lock, and the door opens. Light floods the room from behind him. There he stands. It's John.

I knew I recognised this place. It's John's grandma's house. I haven't actually been in this room before; I suspect this is John's grandma's room, or it was. She's obviously not staying in here now, since my underwear is in her dressing table drawer. I didn't realise where I was at first, but I recognised the painting on the wall straight away. It's a beautiful stone cottage with a thatched roof. I've always loved this house.

We used to visit John's grandma every couple of months. His grandma was always so welcoming, and we really got along. We never slept over, though. John's grandma is very old fashioned and set in her ways. She doesn't believe in sleeping together before marriage, and we respected that, so we just used to come early in the morning and spend the day with her. We had some really lovely times here. Summers in the garden and walking through the forest. Autumn and winter walks. Christmas in the snow. It's beautiful here, but it is also in the middle of nowhere. No one would hear me shouting for help, and to walk to the nearest house or pub, you're talking a thirty-minute brisk walk at best. And that's if I knew which direction to go in.

"Bella, you're up. How do you feel?" he asks.

Is he serious? I just look at him with absolute disgust. He looks like he's lost a lot of weight. He's always been a well-built man who looks after himself, but now he looks gaunt. His skin is pale. His eyes are sunken in, and he's obviously not shaved in weeks.

"How do I feel?! I'll tell you how I feel, John— like I've just been kidnapped by a psycho! What the hell are you playing at?!" I scream.

He walks into the room and goes to sit on the bed beside me. I automatically jump up to get away from him. I put too much weight on my bad leg and fall on the floor. John picks me up sooner than I can protest.

"Hey, calm down—it's me. Your John. I'm not going to hurt you."

Is he for real? I let him lay me down on the bed. I shuffle up the mattress with my elbows and look at him where he is standing beside me.

"I've brought you here so we can try again, Bella. I know you still love me. I've been waiting for you to come to your senses and come home. But in London, there were obviously too many distractions for you. I had to get you away from there."

"John, no—I don't love you anymore. Not like that, anyway, and even less now. God, John what have you done!"

John gets this angry look in his eyes. "You don't mean that, Bella. You're just confused. Once we spend some time alone, you'll remember how good we are together."

"No! Let me go home. It's not going to work. You can't keep me here! And I need to get to the hospital. I think I have broken my ankle and maybe my leg. Please, John I'm begging—let me go!"

I rise up off the bed and hop onto the floor. I push past him and go for the door, but he grabs me by the arms, throws me round, and pins me up against the wardrobe.

"You're... not... going... *anywhere*, Bella," he says with his mouth next to my ear. His breath on my skin sends horrible quivers down my body, and it smells putrid. I'm paralyzed in fear.

"You're mine, Bella. You are going nowhere. Nobody knows you're here—I made sure of that. Mmmm, you smell so good, baby. I've waited so long to have you in my arms again."

He pushes himself against me, and I can feel his erection through his pants. *No, please no.* Sick rises from my stomach, and I let out a sob.

"Sshhhh, don't cry, baby. I know you're not

ready for me yet, but you will be soon."

He licks my ear and down my neck. I'm in a nightmare. Surely this isn't real. This can't be happening. *Oh God, Damien—please come and find me.*

John steps back and looks me up and down. I'm still wearing my white dress from the show.

"I told you not to wear shit like this—you look like a slut!"

He grabs the front of the dress at my chest and rips it from my body. It tears at the seams, giving me painful burns on my sides. It falls to the floor. I'm left standing in my underwear. I cross my arms in front of me. I put my head down and close my eyes to hide my tears. *Please don't let him touch me.*

"Put something decent on. Your things are in the wardrobe," he commands as he walks out of the room. He locks the door behind him.

I slump to the floor and break down.

Crying into my hands, I let my emotions take over for a few minutes. I then get myself together and reach for the wardrobe, using it to pull myself up, and open the doors. Inside are my old clothes. Clothes I left at the house in charity bags when I moved out. There are long frumpy dresses, polo-neck jumpers, long skirts, baggy jeans, and loose T-shirts.

God, why did I used to wear this stuff?

I know why—John.

These are the clothes he wanted me to wear.

I used to kid myself in thinking that I liked to dress this way, but really, I was scared of dressing any other way. I find a brown velour tracksuit, so I put that on with a T-shirt. I sit on the bed when I'm dressed. I'm worn out. The pain in my ankle and leg is getting worse. It's swelling up even more and turning purple.

The best thing I can do right now is play him at his own game. I'll get nowhere arguing with him. I need to get him to let his guard down so I can at least make some kind of attempt at escaping.

I limp over and bang on the door. "John, I am dressed and… I'm sorry. Can we talk?" I may not love him anymore, but I still know him and how his mind works.

The lock clicks and the door opens. John is standing there, looking a bit unsure of what I might do. He's obviously wondering if I'm playing him to get out.

"I'm sorry I got cross with you, John," I try my best to sound sincere. "I was just shocked, and I'm in so much pain with my ankle. It's definitely broken. Would you be able to take me to the hospital, please?"

"No. I can't do that. You can't leave here. It's too risky—sorry."

My heart sinks, even though I didn't expect him to say yes. "How about some pain killers, then? Do you have any ibuprofen or paracetamol?"

"I'm sorry, Bella—I never meant you to get

hurt. But, actually, I don't think it's such a bad thing. Now you're unable to walk, you won't be running off anywhere. It will slow you down. At least until you calm down and see sense. Once you realise how much we belong together, I'll get a doctor to sort you out. I'm sure it will feel better in a day or two anyway."

Okay, so, that tactic's not going to work. "Can I use the bathroom, please? I really need a wee. It's been hours since I last went."

He scrutinizes me, then nods and walks in the direction of the toilet. I try and follow, but I'm struggling to hobble along. He's right—I won't be going anywhere like this.

John turns and looks at me with sympathy. He comes back to me and puts my arm around him, taking my weight. As much as I don't want him near me, I'm glad of the help. We get into the bathroom, and John doesn't leave the room.

"Could you give me some privacy, please?"

"It's nothing I haven't seen before, Bella. Just get on with it."

It's true, I suppose, but I feel incredibly uncomfortable and exposed. I do what I need to do and wash my hands. John then helps me back to the room.

"Do I have to go back in here, John? Can't I sit in the living room with you?"

He thinks about my suggestion. "Not now. I need to make us something to eat. Go and rest, and I'll bring it to you when it's ready."

I am feeling pretty drained—a lie-down does sound like good idea. He helps me back to the bed and locks the door behind him.

I wake from my sleep to John stroking my head. "Hey, sleeping beauty, dinner is served."

I was hoping this was a nightmare I would wake up from, but no—I'm definitely still here.

"I've found some bandages in the bathroom cupboard, so I thought I'd strap your ankle up. It should heal better if it is kept in place. I am sorry about this, Bella. I never meant for you to get hurt," he repeats.

I give John a false smile and nod as he begins to strap up my ankle. Hopefully the support should help with the pain. John helps me into the dining room. He set the table with his grandma's best china and lit the candles in the middle.

"I've made your favourite," he says as he places a plate in front of me. It's steak and peppercorn sauce with potatoes and vegetables. I wouldn't say it was my favourite, but it's what John always used to make us when it was a special occasion. Mainly because it's all he can cook.

"It looks delicious, John—thank you."

I'm not actually hungry, but I know it's been a while since I ate, and I need to keep my strength up. Plus, I need to keep John sweet until I decide what I am going to do.

While John is distracted with eating and making small talk, I try and look for anything that could help me. There must be a phone somewhere.

I know his grandma used to have one, although John has probably removed them all. I can see the phone line socket under the window, but there's nothing plugged into it. There's another large window in here. It looks easy enough to get out of. The trouble is, I don't know what I'd do once I got out. I need to get his car keys. I'd be no use on foot, the nearest house is too far away to walk in my state. But if I could get in a car, I'd have a chance. I just need to get away from here, away from him. That's my plan for now, —find out where his car keys are.

I manage to eat most of my meal, feeling a little more positive that I have some sort of plan. John has opened a bottle of wine, which could be a good or bad thing. Bad, as I know he's more aggressive when he's had a drink, but also good, as he sleeps like a baby when he's drunk. John usually won't stop at one bottle, either, so it looks like I'm in for an interesting night.

We settle into the living room. The television is on—it's "8 Out of 10 Cats Do Countdown." We both naturally fall into our old ways of competing against each other in finding words with the most letters and who can work out the maths problem the quickest. We laugh together, and it reminds me that I was happy with John, especially in those early years. He just changed.

I think back to when it started. John had always had a close group of friends since school.

One of them sadly passed away about four years ago—suicide. It hit all his friends really badly, and they all lost touch with one another after that. That's when he started to drink more. The aggression and possessiveness, if that's what you'd call it, slowly built up during the years after that. He used to be so lovely.

I was eighteen when I met him in a club on the dance floor. He asked for my number, and he called me the next day. He was a bit of a ladies' man, a charmer, but always treated me well. We were inseparable, and I loved him so much. I look at him now, though, and he's no longer that person. I feel guilty. I should have got him some help from a counsellor or spoken to the doctor about his drinking or something.

He turns and sees me looking at him. I force a smile.

"See, Bella? I knew it wouldn't take long for you to realise. Look as us, together and happy. This is where you belong—with me." He drains his glass of wine, gets up, and goes into the kitchen for another bottle.

He's starting to relax a little more around me, I notice; this is good. The more relaxed he is, the greater chance I have of finding his car keys. When we lived together, we had a fruit bowl in the kitchen. We used to put our keys in that. I need to get in there and have a look. I hop up and make my way to the kitchen.

John dashes out and grabs my arm. "Bella

what are you doing?!"

Okay, maybe he's not that relaxed around me just yet. "I changed my mind. I would like a glass of wine if that's okay?"

His face softens. "Of course. Now you sit back down, and I'll get it for you."

He leads me back to the sofa, and I sit down. I may not have made it into the kitchen, but I did see the fruit bowl on the kitchen worktop. No keys, though, unfortunately.

My next thought is his coat pocket. I haven't seen any coats lying about, but there is a cloakroom by the front door. I'd have to go past there to get to the toilet. I doubt he will let me go on my own, but I can try.

"John, I'm just going to nip to the loo!" I shout into the kitchen.

"No! I mean, I'm coming—I'll help." He runs in and grabs me.

"I'm fine, really. I'll hop."

He doesn't say anything else, just leads me down the hall. I don't want to push him, as he might get suspicious. We go past the cupboard near front door; it's ajar, and I can see John's coat hanging in there. It's one I bought him a couple of Christmases ago. I bet the keys are in the pocket.

He guides me into the bathroom, saying, "I'll be right outside. Shout if you need me," and closes the door.

Okay, well, that's an improvement—he left me alone. Baby steps. I need to just wait for my opportunity. It might be tonight, it might be in a few days, but I will get out.

Chapter 19

Damien

We've arrived in the Lake District. We've got the registration plate and make of the second car Bella was taken in. We've followed it up to the lakes, but there aren't many cameras up here, so we still haven't got an exact location. I have rounded up the biggest search-and-rescue team I can. All my available team, the police, the Lake District Search and Mountain Rescue team. I've even called in another favour from Mr. Graves; he's sent me some of his men too. There's a lot of ground to cover.

After I've given everyone their orders and they're all equipped with a first-aid pack and some sort of knife (I insist on this, as she will probably be tied up, but I also want everyone to have some sort of weapon), I send them on their way.

My phone rings—it's Chloe.

"Damien, I've managed to get a message to the airline John's parents are flying with, but they said they didn't check in or board the plane. It doesn't make sense. I've been ringing their house, but there's no answer. I'm on my way there now. I'm thinking a neighbour may have a key and there might be an address book with John's grandma's address in."

"Good idea, but don't go on your own, though—I'll have someone come with you."

"It's okay, Josh has already given me a bodyguard," she says sarcastically

"Good. Stay with him and keep me posted. Ring as soon as you arrive."

"Will do. Be careful Damien, and please find my best friend," Chloe sobs into the phone.

"Have no doubt, I will."

I end the call and climb into the helicopter. I'm looking for the car. It's going to be like trying to find a needle in a haystack in the pitch-black and woodland, but that doesn't mean it's impossible.

We scan the area for a few hours using the thermal night-vision camera. We've covered quite a good area as we stay high up to hopefully not alert Bella's kidnapper that we are close by. There's a clearing in an extensive, dense woodland with a small cottage in the middle. We have flown over plenty of other similar houses, but I just have a gut feeling about this one. We circle the area a couple of times and see a car on the driveway that from up here looks like the one we are searching for. I need to get on the ground for closer look. We land about three miles away. Hopefully they won't have had any warning I'm on my way.

My phone rings—it's Chloe again.

"We've arrived. We didn't need to go to

the neighbours, as the front door was unlocked. They're dead, Damien. Both of them. They've been shot. He's got a gun. You need to find her, please!" Chloe cries down the phone.

Josh asked Mike to stay with Chloe, and he comes on to the line. "Boss, I've located their address book, and I have a Lake District address for 'Mum.'"

I crosscheck the address he recites with our coordinates, and bingo. We are here. I waste no time in heading towards the house.

Bella

It's well into the early hours now, and John is very relaxed and pretty drunk. We've reminisced about old times—well, John has. I've smiled and nodded along. I have had some good times with John, but not this John. When I get out of here, I'm going to get John the help he needs. I know the old John is in there somewhere—he just needs help finding himself.

I look over at him, and he's falling asleep in the chair. This could be my opportunity. I wait for him to start snoring to ensure he's in a deep sleep.

My heart starts to race, and my ears start to ring. I need to do this now. I get up quietly and slowly make my way out of the living room and into the hall. I use the walls and furniture to support my weight. I get to the cupboard and pull the door open. It makes a loud screeching sound as do. I freeze and listen. John has stopped snoring. I hold my breath and pray he hasn't fully woken.

After a minute or so, he begins to snore again. Thank goodness. I reach into the cupboard and grab John's coat. It feels heavy, like there's something in the pocket. I put my hand in and feel keys. Thank the Lord. I put the coat on, as it's one less thing to carry, and I get to the front door. I unlock the bolts and chain. I try a few keys until the door opens. I sigh in relief and take a deep breath. I've done it.

I put the keys back in the pocket and make my way to the car. My leg is so painful, but I use it anyway. I run as fast as I can. I pull out the keys and look for the car key. It's not here. There's no car key on this key ring. I search through the pockets. Nothing. I let out a cry and drop to my knees. This can't be. I was so close! Why is the car key not here?! Why did I not check? I mentally kick myself.

I'm suddenly brought out of my self-annoyance by the sound of movement in the house. He's awake. Shit. All I can do is run.

I head down the driveway and then into the woods on the right. If I can try and head in the direction of the drive, I should find my way the main road. I need to keep deep enough in the woods that John won't see me from the road, though.

It's pitch-black and freezing. I'm glad I put John's coat on, but I can still feel the icy air. The undergrowth of the woodland is dense and comes up to my knees in some areas. It's incredibly hard to walk in, never mind run. My broken ankle is on fire, and my feet are stinging from constant cuts and puncture wounds with each step I take. My adrenaline is wearing off now, and I am very aware that I am barefoot. I'm panting, and my lungs burn as I try and fill them with oxygen.

I hear John shouting my name in the distance. Oh no. He knows I am gone. The distance between us is not enough—I must keep moving.

I don't know how long I've been out here. I'm now crawling and dragging my leg behind me. My body gives up before my mind does, and I go face first into the ground. I lie still and realise I'm numb. I can't feel any pain, just heat rising up my body. I'll just lie here and rest for a moment, then I'll carry on.

I'm woken by the sound of footsteps crunching in the undergrowth. I think about shouting; maybe it's someone who can help me? No, I decide. No one is coming. No one will find me here. I see a torch in the distance—it's coming closer. I need to move. I try to get up, but all I can do is crawl. But I do it—I crawl as fast as I can. The footsteps get louder and faster. I push my body as hard as I can, but it's not enough. He is getting closer. He is going to be so mad. Am I going to die?

Chapter 20

Bella

He grabs me by my hair and pulls me to a standing position. Angling my face next to his, he says, "You little bitch. I knew I couldn't trust you. You'll pay for this, Bella." He smashes my head into a tree, and I'm out.

At some point, my eyes dart open with stinging pain. I must have been out for a while. I see John beside me. I try and move, but I'm tied to the bed. My wrists and ankles are fastened to each bed post. I am wearing only underwear. John is cleaning the wounds on my legs and feet. My body doesn't look like my own. My legs are covered in blood and bruises. My attention is caught by my leg and ankle. My shin bone is visibly piercing through my skin it seems it wasn't only my ankle that was broken, no wonder I am in so much pain. I throw up at the sight.

John shouts, "For fucks sake, Bella, don't you think I've got enough to clean up? Look at the fucking state of you! Look what you have done to yourself! This is all your fault!"

He pushes off the bed and lunges towards me. He's got a gun in his hand. I do not know this man in front of me. John has never even held a gun. Where on earth would he get one from? He holds it to my head. I scream and close my eyes. In this moment, I want him to kill me. I want to die. I have no fight left.

BANG! I hear the sound of a gun. Thank God. He's done it. He's killed me. The nightmare is over.

I wait for the pain to disappear, but it doesn't. I still feel everything. Surely not. Surely in death there is no pain and everything is black? I expected white fluffy clouds and golden gates. I realise my eyes are still closed. I slowly open them, apprehensive at what I might see. To my surprise, I see familiar, comforting eyes. The eyes are Damien's. But they're different to how I've ever seen them before. They're full of pain and concern.

"Damien, you're here?"

"Yes, I am, my Bella."

And then it comes. The pain subsides and the bright lights take me away.

Damien

I work my way through the woods as fast as I can. I reach the house and see the car. It's definitely the one we've been looking for. The back light is half hanging out. The bastard had her in the boot. I quietly creep up to the house. I want to sneak up on him. I'll have the best chance of saving Bella if I catch him off-guard. But I then hear her scream, and my logic is gone.

I storm through the house, following the sound of the scream. I see him bending over her. I grab him, put my gun to his temple, and pull the easiest trigger of my life. I throw him behind me and kneel at the side of the bed. My heart breaks at the sight of her.

Her beautiful body is unrecognisable. She's tied to the bed in her underwear. I regret giving him such an easy death. I now want to torture him like he's done to my Bella. I stare at her, hoping she's still alive. I'm too scared to touch her.

Then her eyes flutter, and relief overcomes me.

"Damien, you're here?" she says.

"Yes, I am, my Bella," I tell her, but my heart breaks. She didn't think I would come? I took too long. How could I have let this happen to her? Bella's eyes roll back, and her body goes limp.

I radio through. "Josh! I need the helicopter and paramedics here ASAP!"

"They're on the way, Damien."

"I've found her, Josh. I've found her!"

I hear the helicopter and sirens. "It won't be long now, my Bella. We will have you fixed up and home in no time."

I need to untie her, but first, I need to sort the situation. I wipe the gun and place it in John's hand and press his finger around the trigger. I then leave it on the floor beside him. I take a couple of photos on my phone for my own evidence, and then I untie Bella.

I find a clean blanket in the wardrobe and wrap her in it. I take her into the living room where there are no bits of brain covering the walls. The paramedics come in, followed by Josh and the police. The paramedics want to take Bella from me, but I won't let her go. They treat her in my arms, and then I carry her to the helicopter where they secure her on to a stretcher. I hold her hand for the entire journey to the hospital. The paramedics work hard giving her all the treatment they can. Her pulse is faint, but she has one. Thank goodness. My Bella is strong and determined, and I know she will get through this.

When we get to the hospital Bella is whisked away for emergency surgery. It kills me to not be at her side.

I sit in the family waiting room with her parents and Chloe. There are people coming in and out of the room. People are talking, but I can't speak. It's taking all of my energy just to breathe. I stare at floor with my head in my hands. My legs bounce up and down. I just can't take it. Her life is in someone else's hands, and I can't do anything about it. Sitting here is driving me mad. I need to get out. I feel guilty and helpless.

I stand up and push past everyone lingering in the doorway and the hall. I need some air.

Josh follows me out and asks, "How're you doing, mate?" He puts his arm around my shoulder.

I shrug it off. I can't do comfort right now. I need to break something. There's a glass bus shelter beside me, so I put my fist through it. The pain brings me back to some reality.

Josh takes off his jacket and wraps it around my fist. "Look, mate, I can't begin to imagine how you must be feeling right now. I saw it with my own eyes. We've seen some shit over the years, but this is up there with the worst. But none of this was your fault. If it wasn't for you, she would still be there, or worse. You found her, Damien, and she's going to be okay."

Josh knows me well. He knows what goes on in my head.

"Guys, the doctor's here, and he's got an update on Bella. They're waiting for you." We follow Chloe back to the family room.

"Bella is now in recovery. She had a bleed on her brain that we successfully stopped and a fracture to her skull. Her leg and ankle had many fractures that have now been pinned back into position. She's been through a lot mentally and physically. We have given her a lot of painkillers, which will make her sleep and give her body chance to recover. I am extremely hopeful that she will make a full recovery."

The doctor turns to me. "Mr. King, that was a great effort on your part, and it seems you got there just time. She is a very lucky lady."

"I'm the lucky one, I can assure you, doctor.

And thank you for everything you have done." I shake his hand with as much gratitude as I can.

There's a sigh of relief as the doctor leaves the room. Everyone seems to relax a little, except for me. I can't shake the guilt.

"Damien, thank you for saving our daughter. I will forever be in your debt," a tearful Henry says as he taps my back. I do not feel worthy of thanks.

It's been twenty-four hours since Bella was admitted, and I haven't left her side. Her entire family has been here, and they've finally gone home, leaving me alone with Bella.

I sit at her side, staring at her beautiful face. She has a large purple bruise from the top of her forehead over her right eye and down to her cheek bone. She has a cut through her eyebrow which has been stitched back together. The rest of her face has little cuts and bruises marring her perfect skin. I feel a range of emotions. The sense of not being in control is having the greatest effect on me. All I can do is sit here and hold her hand, waiting for her to wake up. She looks so peaceful now. The nightmare will start again once she awakes.

Nobody yet knows what happened to Bella while she was in the hands of that monster. Although she was only gone for about twelve hours, her injuries show what an intense and horrendous ordeal she has endured.

There's a tap at the door, and I look up to see Josh in the doorway. "Hey, mate, can I have a word?"

I nod and follow Josh down the hall to an empty family room.

"I've had a meeting with the police this morning," Josh begins, his voice bearing a tone that worries me. "It seems that John was actually employed by King Security and that is how he got to Bella. He was one of the new security recruits we took on a few weeks ago. He was covering backstage. I'm so sorry, Damien. All his credentials checked out. I checked his references and police records—he was totally clean. He used his real name. I just didn't know who he was."

My heart drops to my gut. No, Josh wouldn't know who John was. But I would have. If I had read John's application, I would have known straight away. Only I didn't read it. Josh asked me if I had wanted to go through them before he interviewed, but I didn't. I've let myself slip. I have let my emotions take control, and in doing so, someone I love got hurt. This could have been prevented. I could have stopped this.

"You weren't to know, Josh, but I should have. You asked me to look over them, but I didn't."

"Damien, don't—"

I interrupt him. "Leave it, Josh. I'm going home for a shower. Will you stay with Bella until her parents return? I don't want her being alone."

"Of course."

I get a taxi to the nearest pub. I order a bottle of scotch, much to the barman's surprise, but he gives it me anyway. I find a table and sit in a quiet corner of the old-fashioned pub. I'm trying to process the information Josh has just told me. I knew we had tight security on the event. I couldn't understand how John had managed to get in. Although I'd not really thought much of it yet, as my mind has been solely on Bella. Now I know how he got to her. He had been there all the time.

I drain my glass and refill it.

How could I have let this happen? Nothing ever gets past me. I make a vow to myself now. I will do all I can to ensure Bella is never hurt again, no matter what the consequences. My mind wanders back to Pete's words to me at my father's funeral. If he finds out about my love for Bella, he will no doubt try to harm her.

I sit and think until my brain hurts and my bottle is empty.

"All right, pal, I've ordered you a taxi. It's waiting outside," says the barman, who's standing at my table.

I've seen him keep checking on me, and he obviously thinks it's time for me to go. I've no objections.

Somehow, I make it into my bed after the taxi drops me home. I'm still fully clothed, but I cannot function any longer. I close my eyes. The room is spinning. The contents of my stomach, pretty much the whole bottle of scotch, projectiles out of me and across the bedroom floor. I don't care in the slightest. I wipe my mouth on the bedsheet and fall into a deep sleep.

Chapter 21

Damien

I'm walking down a long hallway; there's a light the end, and I know I need to get to that light. I run as fast as I can, but the light doesn't seem to get any closer. I push with all my might. I run and run, and this time, I finally I reach a bright yellow door. I turn the handle and it opens. There right in front of me is what I have been searching for my whole life, the final piece of my puzzle. I reach out to touch... but I'm pulled back with such force, the light disappears in front of me. My body becomes heavy, and I'm now in darkness. I saw it. I saw what I need to be free. But it's gone. I don't remember what it was.

My mouth feels like sandpaper, my head has a banging pulse of its own, and I can smell a putrid stench which turns my delicate stomach. Snippets of memories return. I groan at the reality of the nightmare I am currently in. I need to get out of this room.

I have a shower, then go into the kitchen and make myself a strong coffee. I sit for what must be an hour, as when I take a sip of my coffee, it is stone cold. I feel out of control, and it is so very foreign to me.

I hear my lift arrive. I know who it is; only two people know my access code, and one of them is lying in hospital. "What are you doing here?" I grumble to Josh as he steps out of the lift.

"I came to see if you're still alive. I've been worried, mate. It's been twenty-four hours since I saw you at the hospital. Your phone goes straight to voicemail. What the hell have you been doing?

"Want one?" I lift my coffee to Josh.

"Yeah, go on, then."

I make Josh and myself each a fresh coffee, and we sit at the kitchen island.

"You need to snap out of this, Damien. I know you're blaming yourself, but none of this was your fault, and if it wasn't for you, things would be a lot worse."

I don't say anything. I just stare into my coffee. It *is* my fault. I could have prevented it.

"Bella's awake, and she's asking for you."

Those words constrict my chest. I want nothing more than to be by her side. Knowing she's asking for me breaks my heart. But I cannot go. Not yet. I must stay away until I figure out what is going on in my head and am sure Bella is safe. I cannot put her at any more risk. Josh is right—I need to snap out of it. I need to get back to my old, controlled self.

Josh's phone rings, and he answers it with a question that catches my attention, bringing me out of my anger and self-pity. "What's the situation?" He stands up, his face serious as he listens. "We will be there as soon as we can. Keep us updated. "Get your kit. We are leaving," he says to me as he looks around for his keys.

"What's going on?!" I demand.

"There's a fire at the hospital. Mike radioed in for back up. He's been watching Bella. When the backup arrived at Bella's room, the hall was filled with smoke, and Mike was unconscious on the floor. He's been stabbed. Bella's bed is empty. The hospital has been evacuated, and they won't let anyone other than the firefighters in."

This can't be happening. Am in a fucking nightmare?!

"Suck it the fuck up, and let's go save your girl!" Josh demands as he stares into my eyes and squeezes both my shoulders.

It's all the encouragement I need; adrenaline rushes through my body.

We get some equipment from my office. Weapons and fire equipment. I get another phone, which is charged, and I put my SIM card in. On the way down to the car, I hear message after message arrive as my SIM registers in the phone. I've got my work head on now—it's the only way I'll get through this. We set off at speed, and I take out my phone, preparing myself for what's about to come. I've numerous messages from Josh, Mike, Bella— but I can't read those. I need to stay focused.

An unknown number has sent three messages.

Unknown: I TOLD YOU I WOULD MAKE YOU PAY!

And there's a picture of Bella asleep in her hospital bed.

Unknown: **MEET ME ON THE ROOF. COME UNARMED AND ALONE.**

These were sent thirty minutes ago. SHIT!

Another message comes through as I stare at the phone.

UNKNOWN: WAITING!

And a photo of Bella on the ground, looking extremely vacant and pale.

My adrenaline rises again. I read the messages to Josh, and we come up with our strategy. He phones the team to prepare them, and we are ready when we arrive at the hospital. *I'm coming for you, my Bella.*

Bella

I've been in and out of consciousness all day. Well, I think it's the daytime—I'm never sure how long I've been out. I'm feeling pretty numb. Everyone is fussing around me—Mum and Dad especially—asking me how I feel and what I remember with such sympathy and care.

I remember everything. From the moment John grabbed me backstage to Damien finding me at the house. I don't feel anything, though. Not fear, not relief, not pain, although I am confused as to why Damien isn't here. I've asked my parents, the nurses, every visitor I've had, and there's been plenty, saying, "Where is Damien? I need him." But everyone just answers with "He will be back soon." I really hope he is okay.

My visitors finally leave me for a while. It's been like a conveyer belt—one lot leaves as the next arrives. I've still got Mike outside the door, but he stays out there, leaving me to get some rest. I fall asleep quickly. The painkillers I'm being fed through the drip in my arm help me rest.

I'm having a nightmare. It's dark. I can't see anything, but I can hear the sound of men fighting, banging noises, fists hitting skin and bone. Then painful screams from a male voice. I wonder if this is a dream or a flashback, but I don't remember any fighting between Damien and John. I then realise my eyes are closed and I am awake. Opening them, I see I'm in my hospital room.

I look at the door where the sounds are coming from. There's a loud thud, and Mike's face is pressed up against the small rectangular window in the door. I gasp in horror. Mike's eyes look right through me, then he slowly slides down. I hear the sound of his body hitting the floor. Maybe this a nightmare? I need to wake up.

I hear scuffling sounds in the hallway. The door opens, and a man holding a blood-stained knife hanging at his side stands staring at me.

"Well, well. Here she is—the one the devil finally let into his heart. I have to say, you're not what I expected you to look like. You're young and pure looking, but maybe that's the attraction?"

I sit frozen in bed. I have never seen this man before in my life. My thoughts go straight to John—maybe he isn't dead like everyone told me he was. Maybe he came back to finish me off. But this definitely isn't John. Has John sent someone to get me? But something tells me not, and I am confused by his words. The devil? I look at the knife in his hand. Blood drips from the blade onto the light blue hospital floor. Panic sets in as I realise that the blood must belong to Mike.

"Get up. You're coming with me."

At this point, there's footsteps in the hallway, then a little scream from a female. She must have seen Mike on the floor. She then appears at my door, and I see it's the nurse who has been looking after me today.

"Bella!" she gasps as she sees the man and registers the scene.

The knife-wielding man shouts at her to leave, which she does. I don't blame her. He would kill her, too—I'm sure of it.

The man takes his backpack off and pulls out a black bottle. He takes the lid off and pushes a rag into it. He walks out into the hall, lights the rag with a lighter, then throws it down the corridor to the left. He runs back in and pulls me out of bed.

"Get off me!" I scream falling to the floor. My IV is ripped from my hand, squirting blood onto my nightgown and the floor.

He puts his arm under my shoulder, lifting

me up. "COME ON!!!"

He drags me out of the room as the fire alarm starts to blare. I have no strength to fight.

I smell petrol and smoke. It's the first time I have been out of bed since I came into hospital apart from a few trips to the loo, held up by the nurse. I can hardly move my legs. They don't feel like my own. One of them has a plaster cast up to my knee and feels like a block of concrete, and the other is like jelly. I scramble to keep up with him, but I don't have the energy, and I flop to the floor. He is shouting at me constantly to "Hurry up", "Move", and "Come on!" He lets go of my arm and wraps my hair around his fist. He then drags me along the floor.

A few people run past us, but they're in such a panic with all the smoke and the fire alarm, they don't take ay notice of me. After dumping me into the lift, the man takes out another bottle, lights it, and throws it out of the lift doors just as they close. I am lying on the floor of the lift when it suddenly stops, and we are in complete darkness. My kidnapper is now frantically pressing all the buttons. The lift must have been switched off with the fire or have been affected by it. You're always told never to use a lift in fire. He fumbles around in his bag, muttering to himself. He gets something out and prises the door open with it.

The lift has stopped between floors. The floor is halfway up the lift doors, and below it is a brick wall. The kidnapper flings his bag up out of the doors and onto the floor above. He then does the same with me.

"Ahh!" I cry as my chin hits the floor, and my front teeth collide with it, too, breaking one of my top teeth on impact. The pain shoots right up my nose and into my head. I suppose it's the least of my worries right now, though.

"Please stop." But he doesn't.

He again drags me by my hair. It's painful. I feel strands being ripped from my scalp at the root. I am doing my best to get to my feet, but I am so weak.

After what feels like a lifetime of having my whole body weight pulled by my hair and banged and scraped up goodness knows how many flights of stairs, we finally reach the top. The man has his knife out again and holds it out in front of him as he opens a fire exit door at the top of the stairs. He moves us out through the door, and the cold, fresh air hits me. I am only wearing and hospital nightgown, so I'm instantly covered in goosebumps.

We are on the hospital roof. There's a greenhouse to the right. We make our way over and go inside. There are some blankets and cushions on the floor, along with bits of rubbish and an ashtray. It looks like staff maybe come up here for a break. It's definitely warmer in here than outside. I prop up a few cushions for my back and curl up, tucking my legs into me as much as my cast will allow.

"Now we wait," says the man.

I stare at him. I am very confused as to why this is happening to me... again. Maybe it's like in that film "Final Destination" where those people changed seats on the plane and survived the crash when they were supposed to die and then death catches up with them in different ways. Maybe I was supposed to die with John, and this is death's way of putting that right. Who knows, but I am going to ask him.

Chapter 22

Bella

"Who are you? What is going on?" I ask trying to come across stronger than I feel.

The man turns to me and laughs. I finally get a good look at his face, and he's not what I expected him to look like. He is in his thirties, I'd say, not bad looking. He's got medium brown hair that looks like it's been recently cut, short at the sides and longer on top. It looks like he spent time styling it this morning, blow drying it back and spraying it into position, although it is a little dishevelled after the recent event

Strange—I wonder what he was thinking while doing that this morning. He's wearing grey trousers and a grey jacket zipped up to the top. They look brand-new and very thick and heavy—maybe they are fireproof or something. They must be warm, as sweat is pouring from his face.

"Look Mr...? I'm far from scared. You wouldn't believe the stuff I have been through the past few days, so let's just cut to the chase; maybe we can hurry this along. What are we doing up here? And who is the 'devil' you mentioned?"

"You're feisty. Claire was feisty too."

Who the hell is Claire? I wonder, but I don't speak. I just listen and wait for more. He's deep in thought. He looks like he's remembering something happy, then sad, which turns to anger. After a minute or so, he snaps out of it, regaining his control.

"Today is the day I finally get revenge. The day when the devil will finally feel the pain he has caused our family."

"I don't understand—who are we talking about, and what have they done?" I ask, still confused but determined to get to the bottom of all this.

"Damien," he says as if the name pains him.

Now we are getting somewhere. My Damien. Clearly This guy has some vendetta against him. "Okay, so, what has Damien done, exactly?"

The guy seems to grow a couple inches taller, his face turns red, and his expression is evil. "HE MURDERED MY SISTER!"

I am a little taken aback by this. I do not for one second think that this is true, but he obviously believes it is, so I am going to be careful in this situation.

"Oh, my goodness, that's terrible. I am so sorry."

He looks at me, clearly a little surprised by my reaction, bows his head, and starts to calm a little.

"What happened?" I ask.

He stiffens and glares at me. "I am not discussing this with you."

He gets out his phone and types something. I assume it's to Damien. For the first time since this guy entered my hospital room, I feel a little scared. Not for me. Scared for Damien.

I watch him for a few minutes. He's clearly nervous. This is obviously a new experience for him. He keeps checking his phone, and from his reactions, I don't think Damien has even read the messages. Each time he checks, he seems to get a little more panicked.

I try assessing the situation. I don't know this guy from Adam, so I'm not too sure how any of this will go. At least I knew John, so I had some idea how to approach him. There's no chance of me escaping this time (although it didn't do much good last time, come to think of it). I couldn't even keep up with him getting up here, so there's no way I will be able to outrun him. My best and only option is to try and make "friends" with this guy and wait for Damien to arrive.

That's if he does arrive.

He's not been to see me at the hospital since I regained consciousness. Maybe he doesn't want to be in our relationship anymore. Maybe everything with John has made him realise he doesn't want to be in a relationship. This hurts my heart to think about. But there's definitely something going with Damien. We can get through it, I am sure—I just need to see him. Maybe all this with whatever his name is has got something to do with why he hasn't been. I hope he is okay.

"What's your name?" I ask him as he looks at his phone for the hundredth time.

"Pete," he answers straight away on a reflex, then looks at me with a scowl, realising what he has done. He obviously didn't want to tell me that.

"Hello, Pete. I'm Bella, but you already know that."

Pete just looks at me, trying to read me, I think. He sighs and leaves the greenhouse. "Don't move!" he calls at me as he closes the door behind him.

As if I could.

I sit up and watch him through the window. He opens the door we came out of and looks down the stairs. He obviously doesn't see anything, so he shuts it and paces up and down, staring at his phone and biting his fingernails. After a few minutes of working himself up, he comes back into the greenhouse.

"Everything okay?" I ask, giving him a little smile.

He looks at me, confused. Yep, this is my plan—kill him with kindness.

Pete doesn't respond; he bends and gets a rope out of his backpack. He sits in front of me, not saying a word. He takes my hands and ties them together, and he then ties them to my legs. I don't bother to resist. He ties them tight, but he's the gentlest he has been with me. He mutters something under his breath, but I don't catch what it is.

"I will be back soon. Stay here and be quiet," he says without making eye contact.

Pete disappears back into the hospital. He has taken his backpack with him. When he returns about fifteen minutes later, he smells of smoke and petrol. I hope there's a way down from this roof without going back inside.

The pain in my body is beginning to grow, I'm probably due for some more meds.

Trying to ignore my discomfort my thoughts then go to Damien. I hope he doesn't get hurt. I need to do something.

"What is your plan, Pete? Burn the hospital down and kill us all? Just kill me and be killed by Damien or spend the rest of your life in prison?"

Pete looks at me, surprised. I'm not sure if he has thought that far ahead.

So I push. "I can't begin to imagine what you must have gone through or still be going through, but surely your sister wouldn't want you to be doing this?"

Pete storms at me and grabs my hair again. I wince at the pain.

He pulls my head so my ear is next to his mouth "Do not ever talk about my sister. You know nothing. Revenge is the only option now."

Okay, so maybe I pushed a bit too hard. This guy has a screw loose. He's unpredictable and obviously doesn't have much of a plan.

He gets out his phone again and smiles to himself. Damien must have read the messages now or has replied. Pete takes a photo of me and seems to send that too. "Won't be long now, princess!" He smiles to himself.

I feel sick. Damien obviously now knows I'm here. He will have a team sorting out my rescue, I'm sure. I just need to trust him. I can't help but worry, though. I am starting to panic. I can feel my blood pressure rising and my heart racing. Needing to keep myself calm, I close my eyes and put my head between my knees.

I think about all the wonderful things in my life. There's my relationship with Damien, which I hope will be as strong as ever when all this is over. He's a wonderful man. There are my parents, who love me unconditionally and would do absolutely anything for me. I hope they aren't too worried about me. I have already put them through hell with the John situation. Then there's my friends, like my absolute best friend Chloe, without whom I wouldn't be who I am today. All my friends and colleagues at the salon, especially Katie, who made me feel at home from the start. I love my work, which is more of a passion to me. I have so much to be thankful for. Once I get down off this roof top, though, I think I am going to book a holiday. I need a break.

I'm not sure how long I spend lost in my own thoughts, but Pete's behaviour changes, and it pulls me back to reality; something must be going on. Pete grabs my legs and cuts the rope between them, just leaving my hands still tied.

He then pulls me up and drags me out of the greenhouse and onto the roof. The wind has picked up, and I shiver and shake in the cold. Pete puts his left arm around my front, holding my arms down against my body. My hands are tied at my wrists, so I can't really move. I am also realising that I am becoming weaker and weaker by the minute. I think I was running on adrenaline before, and it is quickly fizzling out. I feel very lightheaded.

With his right hand, Pete pulls out his knife and holds it to my throat.

"Please, Pete. Don't do this." I feel his head dip and his hand drop a little, but only for a second, and then it's back up, the cold blade resting below my voice box.

There's a banging sound coming from the door to roof. The door opens with a fast, powerful swing. Smoke comes billowing out of the building. Two large figures appear out of the smoke. They're wearing oxygen masks on their faces, yellow helmets, and thick fireproof suits. I assume they must be firefighters until one takes off his mask and I hear his voice. Damien.

"What the hell are you doing, Pete!?" Damien demands.

"I am finally going to get justice for my sister! You killed her, Damien! You broke my parents' hearts!"

Damien doesn't reply. He just lets him speak.

"We have never been the same since. You ruined our lives, you MURDERER!" Pete is getting angrier. He tightens his grip on me, and the knife pushes into my neck.

Damien's eyes meet mine; he's speaking to me through them. He's asking me to be calm and trust him.

I do, I say back with a tear in my eye.

He understands and puts his eyes back on Pete. "I am sorry, Pete. I never meant for Claire to get hurt."

"DO NOT SAY HER NAME! YOU HAVE NO RIGHT!"

Pete's anger rises even more, and he pushes the knife further into my neck. I feel my skin break under the sharp blade. The release of warm blood runs down my neck on to my chest. I see the pain in Damien's eyes as he looks at me.

"It's me you want, not Bella. Please, Pete, let her go. I will do whatever you want—just let her go. She's done nothing wrong," Damien pleads.

I haven't seen Damien in this position before. He normally has control of every situation, but here he has none, and I know he hates it. I see him like this, and I love him even more. It must be taking all his strength for him not to come over here and beat Pete to a pulp. But he can't— he's protecting me. I see Damien's eyes flicker to his left, just for a second. Has he seen something?

Pete then starts to talk about his sister and their time growing up. How she used to look out for him. I get a glimpse of the man he was before his sister's death. It's horrendous what grief can do to person. I am feeling extremely weak now, my vision is very blurry, and I'm hearing sounds like I am underwater. I feel Pete's anger building again. My legs give way, and I slump to the floor. The knife penetrates my skin again, and I feel another rush of warmth down my neck. It feels good. I am so cold. It warms me up for a moment. I hear Damien shout, and there's a bang as I it the cold hard floor. I am exhausted, so I let my eyes close, and I drift into a deep state of unconsciousness.

Chapter 23

Damien

"He's down!" I shout into my microphone. We had a sniper on the roof next door. They shot Pete in the back of the head. We won't have to worry about him anymore. I push his body away from Bella and assess her situation. She is breathing, thank goodness, and her pulse is a little faint, but it's there. She has two cuts on her neck, the bastard—if he wasn't already dead, I would be killing him now. They're bleeding but seem to be stopping. I think they're surface wounds, thank goodness.

I pull out my first-aid kit and quickly bandage her neck. I wrap her in a fireproof blanket and put a spare oxygen mask on her face. I lift Bella into my arms and carry her back into the building. There's not as much smoke now. The firefighters were putting out the fires when on my way up here, and they have since made good progress. King Security work closely with the fire services as well as the police. We've helped each other out on many an occasion. I take the stairs with ease and stare at my Bella. I am never letting her go now.

There's an ambulance waiting outside, and I get into the back with Bella in my arms. I let them get her stable and then direct them to my home. Kingston Manor. I have already arranged for a medical team to be there waiting for Bella's arrival. I have explained the situation to Penny, and I'm sure she will have sorted out everything else. This time, I will not be leaving Bella for a moment.

Everything is in hand at Kingston. Bella is set up comfortably in my—well, our—room. She has a medical team on hand twenty-four hours a day. Thankfully I have the influence and money to have better care for Bella in my home than any hospital. Bella has a few stitches in her neck and is on some strong antibiotics, as she had the beginnings of pneumonia. Bella's parents and Chloe are also staying with us. Josh is here a lot, too, keeping an eye on things—on one thing, or rather, person, in particular, if I'm not mistaken.

"Hey, my beautiful Bella, how are you feeling?" I say as I walk into our room.

Bella is sitting up in bed, reading. It has been a week since the hospital incident, and she is getting stronger by the day.

"Now that it has quietened down with visitors and you're feeling better, I wondered if we could have a chat? I think I have some explaining to do."

Bella puts her book down and straightens herself in the bed. She takes a deep breath and looks a little worried.

"That's if you're up to it, of course?"

"Yes, it's fine, Damien. Please go on."

I sit on the end of the bed and gather my thoughts. I have known I needed to speak to Bella about Pete and explain. I haven't wanted to upset her or slow her recovery, so I haven't yet discussed what happened with her. I have also been putting it off because I am not sure how Bella feels now and how she will feel after I explain. Bella obviously knows that Pete was angry at me and that he was willing to take her life because of that. She also must know that he blames me for his sister's death, but she hasn't mentioned anything to me about it.

With family and friends visiting the police and the medical team's presence, we haven't really spent any time alone, apart from at night when I get into the sofa bed at the other side of the room while Bella is asleep.

"Okay, well, I am going to start from the beginning." I take a deep breath. "When I was in college, I met a girl called Claire. She was so beautiful—everyone wanted to date her, and unfortunately for her, the only person she wanted to date was me. At the time, I thought it was great. I had what everyone else wanted. After a while, Claire started getting very serious. She was talking about engagements and moving in together. It was definitely not what I wanted. I just wanted to have fun. I tried to explain to her that we were too young for that and we should enjoy life. Claire didn't get the message at all. I even broke up with her a few times, but she still came back. I was young and naïve back then, so I decided the best way to get her to move on was to go with someone else—so I did. I slept with her best friend. I got a friend I had at the time to take photos of us together and email them to her."

I bow my head in self-disgust. Bella looks shocked and saddened by my words but nods to encourage me to go on.

"A couple of days later, I found out that she had committed suicide. She had written a note saying how much she had loved me and that I had broken her heart. That I had also taken away her best friend, and she could no longer live with the pain."

My voice breaks as I finish. I realise I have never actually spoken those words out loud. My family and Josh knew about it all when it happened, but I have never had to explain it to anyone before.

Bella takes my hand in hers and gives me a sad smile. She's about to say something but I stop her.

"Please just let me get it all out while I can." I am not used to talking about my feelings. "Since then, I have never let any woman get close to me. I have never dated or slept with anyone more than twice. To be honest, there's never been anyone I wanted to see more than that until I met you. I have never wanted anyone to be hurt again because of me, but with you, Bella, I just couldn't stay away. I am sorry—I was selfish." My voice breaks again.

Bella moves over to me and wraps her arms around my neck. I put my head on her chest, and she kisses the top of my head. She then lifts my face, kisses me gently on the lips, and wipes the fallen tears from my eyes with her thumbs.

"When you were kidnapped, I completely lost my head. I have never felt pain like that of losing you, and when I found out that I could have prevented it, I realised it was all my fault. I had hurt someone else, and you could have died because of me."

"What do you mean, you could have prevented it?" Bella asks, confused.

"John was working for King Security. He was one of our new recruits, and his first job was the hairdressing event. I literally handed you to him."

"No, Damien—you weren't to know. You cannot blame yourself for this."

"Yes, I can. Josh had asked me to go through the short list of CVs for the new recruits, and I didn't bother. If I had, then I would have seen him. I would have known it was him, and I would have known he was after you. I could have stopped him. We've also discovered it was John who had you drugged the night you were out with Chloe. His first attempt to kidnap you it seems."

Bella stares at me for a moment, taking it all in, and I can tell she is choosing her words carefully. I know there is no going back from this for us. How could she want to be with me when I have put her through this? I will look after her and make sure she is taken care of for the rest of her life, but I won't ask anything of her. I don't deserve to breathe the same air as her.

Bella takes my face in her hands and looks me in the eyes. "Damien, don't you dare blame yourself for this. I knew you were feeling like this. That's why you didn't come to the hospital after I woke up, wasn't it? No, this was the fault of two crazy men, not you. You are my hero, Damien. You are my love."

Staring back into her eyes, I can't quite believe the words she is saying.

"I will not let them take you away from me, Damien—do you hear me? We will get through this together."

Bella climbs out of the covers and sits on my lap, facing me, with one leg on either side of mine. She kisses me with such love, I feel it in my heart. I kiss her back with as much love and passion as I can. Her hands move to my head, and she strokes her fingers through my hair. Our kiss deepens, and our bodies press into each other. I feel my manhood wake up. This is the first time I have been aroused since the hair show. It feels so good to have her in my arms again. I lay us down on the bed side by side with our legs entwined, but then I feel the cast on her leg and suddenly remember.

I pull away. "Bella, we mustn't—your leg, and you need to rest."

"I am not made of glass! I want you. I need to feel you. I need you to make me feel better. I want you now, Damien." She grabs my ass and pulls me into her, wrapping her good leg around my hip.

"Okay, my Bella," I chuckle as I peel off her little excuse for a pyjama top.

I lay her on her back and kneel in between her legs. I take her in for a moment. She's so incredibly beautiful. Golden blonde hair fans out on the bed, framing her face. Those blue eyes I get lost in sparkle as if they're communicating with my heart. Those plump lips that get me hard by the slightest little pout. I trail my eyes down her body. Damn, is she sexy, even with the bandages and plaster cast. I don't think—actually, I *know* there is not a more beautiful woman in the world. I vow in this moment that I will always appreciate her and what she has given me. But enough of the soppy stuff—I will now take her as mine and show her I am her man and that only I can satisfy her needs.

I kiss her face and then down her neck. Taking one of her breasts in my hand, I massage it gently while taking the other in my mouth, sucking and gently biting her nipple. Bella moans in appreciation. I then swap to the other side. I want to make sure every part of her body is taken care of and feels the love and appreciation I have for it. I work my way down her stomach, kissing and tasting her skin. She smells amazing, like strawberries. I run the tips of my fingers down the sides of her body, following my mouth; this must tickle, as Bella wiggles. Her skin covers itself in goosebumps. I love that her body reacts to me this way.

I reach her tiny pyjama pants, remove them in one quick swoop, and fling them over my shoulder. "We won't be needing these."

Bella giggles at my comment. I spread her legs and look at her most intimate area, and by God, it is glorious. It's pink, plump and glistening, ready and waiting for me. What an honour.

"Mmmm, Bella, you are perfect."

Bella smiles at me with such love. I bend down and start with the insides of her legs, giving her featherlike kisses and tickles with my nose. Once Bella gets used to me being here and I hear her breathing quicken with gasps of appreciation, I move to that special place. The one that belongs to me.

Chapter 24

Damien

I swipe my tongue through her slit, gently caressing her clitoris, rotating round and round. Bella's body begins to move with mine in response to the pleasure—this encourages me more. I use my lips, my tongue, and my nose. I absolutely love being able to do this for her. I continue as her body starts to shake. Her legs start to kick a little, and I know she is there. I work faster and apply more pressure, and then I hear it—the sexiest sound in the world: Bella having an orgasm. An orgasm created by me and happening on my face. I am in heaven. I slow to gentle kisses as she comes down.

Once her shaking has stopped, I can no longer control myself. I pull off my shirt and pants and slide into her. Wow. —It's the most perfect fit. I can feel every part of her inside, and it's sexy as hell. I am so hard, I feel like I could burst. I get to work at claiming my territory. My primal instincts kick in, and I need to claim her as mine. I lift her hips and carefully drape her legs around me so I can enter her deeper. Bella lets out a gasp, but I hold her eyes and I know she's okay. I bend to kiss her and make love to her mouth as I'm pushing inside her, massaging her sensitive spot.

When I pull out of her, her body clenches, pulling me back inside. It's a magical feeling that's sending me over the edge. I know I will never get enough of this. We caress each other's bodies until we both cannot hold out any longer. I sense Bella is close, and I am glad, as I am about to lose control.

Bella closes her eyes.

"No, Bella, look at me. Look into my eyes, I need to see you when you come."

She does as I ask. We hold each other's gaze as euphoria overtakes us—the moment when our bodies give each other most intimate love there could possibly be. Our souls connect. We are one.

"I love you," we say in unison, and my heart grows a little bigger.

We hold each other for a while, and then I hear Bella's stomach grumble. It is getting on for dinnertime. "You need to eat. Let's get washed, and then I will make us food."

"Sounds great. Thank you."

I run a bath for Bella. I make sure it's just the right depth and nice and warm with lots of bubbles, just how she likes it. I roll up some towels and put them on the side of the bath so she can rest her plastered leg on them and keep it out of the water. I pick Bella up and carry her into the bathroom.

She giggles a little and puts her arms around my neck. "I love you, Damien."

"I love you, too, my Bella."

I kiss her on top of her head and put her gently in the bath. I get in the shower, and we both get washed. Once we are dried and dressed, I carry Bella down to the kitchen and sit her on a bar stool at the island. I wanted to make something and bring it up to her, but Bella wouldn't have it. She insisted on coming downstairs. I can't blame her, as she must be getting sick of those four walls. I just don't want her to do too much.

I make us some homemade soup and warm crusty rolls, courtesy of the cook, who has kindly been making sure the kitchen is stocked with quick wholesome meals for the whole family.

Speaking of the family, Bella's mother and father come into the kitchen and join us. "Sweetie, you're up. How are you?"

"I'm feeling really good, thanks, Mum. Damien's been looking after me." Bella blushes, obviously remembering exactly how I have just taken care of her.

"Would you like to join us?" I ask Olivia and Henry. "There's plenty to go around."

"Well, if you don't mind, that would be lovely."

They each take a seat at the island, and we are soon joined by Chloe and Josh. They seem to come as a pair now too. We all sit and eat, and before we know it, two hours of chatter and laughter have passed. It's been a long time since this house heard the sound of a family enjoying one another's company. The evening has been just what Bella and I needed. Bella's got more colour in her cheeks, and the sparkles in her eyes are brighter.

After we've all cleared the kitchen, everyone excuses themselves, and I carry Bella upstairs. We get into bed and snuggle into each other. I lie with my head propped up on some pillows and Bella lies with her head on my chest.

"Damien, will you do something for me?"

"Anything. What is it, Bella?"

"Would you come to counselling with me? Don't answer me yet—just think about it. I think it would help us both."

"I will definitely think about it." I kiss the top of her head, and she snuggles further into me. We are both soon fast asleep.

I am here again, running down that hallway, trying to get to that door. I run as hard and as fast as I can. After what feels like ten minutes running on a treadmill floor that hardly moves, I reach the door. I take the door handle in my hand and turn it. I walk into the room. And there it is right in front of me. I see what I have been searching for my whole life. Of course.

But just like that, I am awake again. Every time I have this dream, once I see what I am searching for, I wake up. Only this time, I can remember what I saw behind that door. I can still see it now. She's in my arms. It's my Bella. I finally found her.

Bella.

We are on the way to hospital to get my cast removed. The sun is shining, and I am feeling wonderful. I am almost as good as new health-wise. I am the happiest I have been in my life. Damien holds my hand as he drives. He doesn't even let go to change gear.

"I've been thinking. Now that I am getting my cast off and I am feeling a lot better, I thought I would move back into the hotel."

Damien turns to look at me. He is wearing sunglasses, so I can't read his eyes, but from the expression on the rest of his face, I don't think he is too happy.

"I am very grateful for everything you have done for me, but I don't want to outstay my welcome. I thought maybe next week?"

"No!"

Okay, he's definitely not happy. I don't say anything. I just watch him take a breath.

He moves our joined hands to his mouth and kisses the back of mine. "Bella. My house is your home. You are my home now. I cannot live apart from you. If you would prefer to live in the hotel, then I will come too. But I thought you were happy at Kingston?"

I smile. I was hoping Damien would feel like this. As I do. We haven't actually had the conversation about future living arrangements, but I know where I want to be, and that is anywhere Damien is.

"Are you asking me to move in with you, Damien?"

His face relaxes as he realises, he doesn't have a fight on his hands. "Yes, I am. Although I didn't think I needed to ask. I thought it was quite clear," Damien answers grumpily.

I squeeze his hand and give him a big smile. "I just didn't want to assume and for you to think I was taking advantage. You have a beautiful home, but I would live on the street as long as it was with you."

"I can assure you we will never be sleeping on the street. And you, my Bella, can take advantage of me however you wish." He raises his sunglasses and gives me a wink.

I melt, feeling like the luckiest girl in the world. .

Epilogue

Bella

It's been twelve months since I was taken by John and Pete. I've now made a full recovery.

I'm back in work at the salon, which is now Bella Hairdressing. Damien kicked out Rebecca along with the franchise and put the sign over the door while I was still in hospital. I don't remember much from the ordeal. I've plenty of scars to remind me, but they're all fading now.

The whole thing has affected Damien just as much as me. Damien has been wonderful. He has taken such good care of me. I've had the best doctors and nurses and every treatment from counselling and psychotherapy to Indian head massage and pedicures. Damien did not leave my side. He comes to the salon with me most days and works from there. He's turned one of the treatment rooms into his office. It was the only way he would let me go back to work.

Mike is back at the door and the salon is busier than ever. Mike, thank goodness has made a full recovery. He had a good few stab wounds and almost died, but thankfully he is now "fitter than ever" (his words). Mike wanted to come straight back to work, so here he is.

Chloe has moved to London. She's living with us until she finds a place of her own. I am hoping something will happen between her and Josh. There is definitely chemistry there.

I've never been happier. I also have a little surprise in store for Damien tonight. I found out I was pregnant yesterday, and as it is his birthday today, I thought I'd make it one of his surprises. Life couldn't be more perfect—with Damien by my side, I will want for nothing more.

Damien.

Today is my birthday, and there is only one thing I want today—and that is for Bella to say she will be my wife. We are going for a meal at our favourite restaurant. I know, however, that she has also invited many of our friends and family as a surprise. Nothing gets past me. But that couldn't be more perfect, really, as I have a surprise for Bella. I am going to ask her to marry me.

First, though, I have my counselling appointment. I have been coming to see Dr. McGrain for about twelve months now. It was Bella's idea. We come together and also separately. It has really helped me. I didn't realise how just talking about how you feel and what goes on in your head can make you feel and deal with situations much better.

I enter Dr. McGrain's room and sit in the chair with a smile on my face, thinking about Bella and this evening.

"Damien, you look particularly happy today. Is there a reason for this?"

"There is. Today is my birthday and the day I am going to ask Bella to marry me."

"Well, yes, I can see why you would be happy today. Many happy returns. And a proposal? That is fantastic news. Do you think you are both ready for this commitment?"

"I do," I answer quickly and firmly, as I have no doubt in my mind.

"How does Bella make you feel, Damien?"

I think for a moment and then smile. "She makes me feel like I have remembered everything," I reply, and I laugh.

It's true. For years, whenever I left a room, I felt as if I had forgotten something. I never usually had, but that's how I felt. But now, I never feel that way. Even if I have forgotten something, I never realise it. As long as I have Bella in my life, I literally have all I need.

On the way to the restaurant, we get stuck in unusually heavy traffic.

"Oh no, we are going to be late, Damien."

"Don't worry, my Bella," I give her hand a squeeze and place it on my leg. "I'll ring through to the office and see if I can find out what is going on. Then we can take an alternative route."

"Hey, boss. What can I do for you? Isn't it your night off?"

"Yeah, we are on our way to my celebration, but we are stuck on Waterloo Street. Do you know where the accident is so we can do a detour?"

"It's not an accident, boss—we've just had a call through. There has been a shooting at a youth centre. A number of casualties, unfortunately."

"Not Christchurch youth centre?" Bella asks.

"Yeah, that's the one."

"Oh God, Damien. That's where Chloe works. She is working tonight."

"Don't worry my Bella, I'll call Josh now. Chloe will be fine, we will make sure of it." I promise, hoping we are not too late.

The End

The story continues in I've Found Her part 2

About The Author

Joy Mullett

Joy Mullett has turned her obsession with reading into writing. Being a lover of romance with a big imagination Joy writes exciting and thrilling stories which are impossible to put down.

Follow Joy on Instagram and Tiktok for her latest releases

Printed in Great Britain
by Amazon